VeriTales: Note of Hope

Veri Tales ®

Note of Hope

Short Stories for the Evolving Spirit

Edited by Helen Wirth

Fall Creek Press
Fall Creek, Oregon

> Fall Creek Press
> Post Office Box 1127
> Fall Creek, Oregon 97438

Library of Congress Cataloging-in-Publication Data

VeriTales : Note of Hope : short stories for the evolving spirit / edited by Helen Wirth.
   Contents: A very safe man / by Bruce Burrows - - The price of limes in Managua / by Susan K. Ito - - Pearl, shadow and light / by John D. Nesbitt - - Elevator up / by Janet Schumer - - Four in the blast / by Judith Davey - - Becoming the chief / by Tom Traub - - Family tree / by Robert U. Montgomery - - Harvest / by David E. Shapiro - - A quality piece / by Brenda Rickman Vantrease - - Maura's vision / by Nina Silver.
   ISBN 0-9632374-2-X (pbk. : alk. paper) : $14.95
   1. Spiritual life—Fiction.   2. Short stories. American.
I. Wirth, Helen, 1931-
PS348.S5V45   1993
813' .0108382—dc20   93-13270
                                                      CIP

Printed in the United States of America

Text and cover printed on recycled, acid-free paper

Table of Contents

Trapped together in an underground shelter, four diverse people brace themselves against terror and their own mortality. They are isolated from the world, but a worse isolation unfolds before them.

Mother Hatchet has been in charge long enough. Johnson Paul knows she has The Power, but he is sure that he can take her place— as soon as he learns enough. He just doesn't know how much is enough.

Michael was unmoved by his father's death, but he grieved the loss of a tree. Now, he struggles to come to terms with how he could possibly have loved the one and not the other.

They long for a child. And the dark reaper, whose scythe has cut through all of history, is about to strike their lives. First harvest is ever the sacrifice.

Alice is only nine, and she is thinking of doing a "bad" thing. But somehow she knows that if she doesn't do it, something far worse is going to happen. There comes a point at which the small world of a child must confront the values of a larger world.

They are her friends—more than friends—and
she wants to help them. But they live in a
dimension separate from her own . . . almost.

A Very Safe Man

A Veri-tale by Bruce Burrows

*Bill Blund's doorbell rang at 8:30 Saturday morning,
catching him conscious.* He had gone to bed early the
night before, his Friday night having been its usual
empty self. Haphazardly wrapped in a bathrobe, and
cradling his coffee mug, Bill staggered to the door of
his small apartment and fell against the peephole. A
clean-cut man. Nice but nondescript suit, rather
young, good looking in the distorted wilderness of the
hall. *Great. Early morning solicitors again. What is it
this time: candy bars? magazines? God?* Bill wondered
when these people would figure out that one reason
Jesus lasted as long as he did was that he didn't spend
his time waking people up on Saturday mornings.

The doorbell again, echoing among the furniture.

"Go away."

"Mr. Blund?" The voice was quiet, polite, confident. Bill didn't remember them ever knowing him by name before.

"Go away. I'm going to church tomorrow. I promise." He turned away from the door.

"Yes, sir, Mr. Blund, but I'm not from the church. I'm from the IRS. May I come in?"

Bill stopped and turned slowly back to the door, a feeling in his stomach like being on a date gone bad and running into an old lover. Bill turned it over in his mind. The IRS? He had filed on time, told the truth. An audit? No, they have to tell you by mail, don't they? Maybe it was just a math problem, like he forgot to carry a one. Or a ten. Probably just a math problem.

"Mr. Blund?" Again, quiet and strong.

"Just a second." Bill drew back the bolt and opened the door.

"Thank you, Mr. Blund. I am sorry to disturb you at this early hour. May I come in?" Bill nodded numbly as the young man entered. Too polite to be from the IRS.

"I paid my taxes. On time, too. Every word was true." He took a sip of his coffee, which had already disintegrated to lukewarm.

The visitor smiled briefly. "I have no doubt of that, sir. That's one of the reasons I'm here."

"So the Internal Revenue Service sent you to thank me?"

Again, the smile. "I'm sorry if I didn't make myself clear, sir. The IRS I represent is not the Internal Revenue Service."

Bill's eyes began to hurt in a way that made him wish he had been drinking last night, so there would at least be an excuse. He went to the kitchen and filled his mug, sat down in the living room across from the man. He lighted a cigarette, leaned back on the couch, and did his best to look exasperated, but the intruder struck back with that damn smile. "Who do you represent, then?" Bill said, deciding to switch to terse.

The visitor slipped into gear. "Mr. Blund— William—May I call you William?"

"Bill."

"Very well. Bill. My name is Kessler, James Kessler, and I represent an organization known as the International Resistance to Solidarity, or IRS. We have been observing you for some time, and we think you would be very interested in our organization."

"Observing? You've been spying on me?"

"No, sir. Spying is prying. We leave that to the government. We have merely talked to a few of your acquaintances and colleagues, observed you at work and in a few social situations, and reviewed all information concerning you that is on file with federal and state agencies. But no spying. May I tell you a bit about the purpose of our organization?"

Bill cursed to himself. Little bastard tricked his way in. Now he had to let him talk. Just like the God people. Once they're in, just let them talk and nod a lot; they'll be gone faster than if you fight them. He decided it was his time to pay for poor early morning judgment. "Sure," he said.

"Thank you." Mr. Kessler adjusted himself in his chair, looking very much the teacher. "Bill, there are basically two types of people in the world: those who act and those who don't. Our organization grew out of those who don't. For years, we have seen world governments rise, fall, evolve, and die. There are always people with new twists on the concept of governing, but those, too, fail. We understand that it is this constant influx of attempted improvement that's the problem."

Bill gloated quietly to himself. This was going to be short. He had caught Mr. Kessler. "You're a Nazi."

Kessler shook his head. "No sir. The Nazis were a new twist on fascism, but they failed as well. You see, Bill, any form of government is tyranny of some form or another. Fascism is simply a more blatant example. But democracies, theocracies, monarchies, all have some weapon of tyranny, whether it is the constraints of liberty, the fear of God, or simply the numbing power of charisma. Tyranny is intrinsic to the nature of government."

Bill sighed. "Okay, the country is going to hell. Big news."

Again, Kessler shook his head. "On the contrary. We're very happy with this nation."

"Okay, now back up a second. You say that all these new ideas fail, all these movements fail, yet you're trying to recruit me into yours. How do you explain that?"

Kessler smiled, as if he had expected the question. "That's the point, Bill. We are the official non-doers. We pride ourselves on not rocking the boat."

"What does that mean?"

"Simply that we accept the fact that tyranny is a part of government. We believe that by this acceptance, society benefits as a whole." Kessler could see by Bill's face that things were still a bit murky. "You see, Bill, while all government is tyranny, there are two basic types of tyranny. There is the tyranny that grows out of well-intentioned, institutionalized governments like our own. This is a subtle tyranny that few truly notice, and those that do simply turn it into parlor room whining. In societies such as these, people are often unhappy, but they attribute it to the times, or their spouse, or the current war. The government, and therefore the society, is safe. Not perfect, but safe.

"Then, there are the tyrannies that grow out of the believers—the driven, idealistic individuals. Why are they driven, Bill? Because they are not content. And they are not content because they are not capable of being content. If they do rise to power, what happens? History has shown us! In addition to the trauma of their initial rise, the turbulence of attempted change causes even more problems, and eventually they are forcing their ideas on the society they sought to change, making people more miserable than they were originally. Look at history! How many revolutionaries became tyrants, and bloody ones at that?"

The argument made Bill uncomfortable. "But what about progress? I mean, I still want things to get better, you know."

The well-practiced smile crossed Kessler's face. "Another common misconception, Bill. But idealistic change is not necessary. Progress will occur. Look at our nation. Look at the innovations we have produced! Television, laser discs, fax machines, microwaves, the fast food franchise. No revolution brought these about! These were brought about by doers—doers who had little concern for government and didn't waste their energy quibbling over who got what rights to free press or fair trial. Our organization supports this. We are organized apathy. We do our jobs, buy the necessary appliances, attend or don't attend church as appropriate, support our military unconditionally. We are the core of the nation. Our membership now numbers over two hundred million nationwide."

Bill choked on his coffee. "Two hundred million? That's impossible! I've never even heard of you!"

"Of course you haven't, Bill. If we advertised our existence, with as many members as we have, we would become a political force. That would run contrary to our purpose. But as the truly silent majority, we maintain our way of life. As long as our members agree to take no political action, or, at the very least, none contrary to the current disposition of the government, we guarantee a steady job, a mortgage, health insurance, and a valid credit card. We take care of our own."

"What does all this have to do with me? Why are you telling me this?"

Kessler's smile gave way to a small laugh. "Don't you see, Bill? You are perfect for our organization. We checked. You have a college degree, but have worked outside your field in the same job for eight years. You file your taxes every year, never lie, and always give a dollar to the campaign fund, though you almost never vote; and when you do, it's always straight party line— Democrat, incidentally, just as your parents were. In the past five years, you have purchased a computer, a CD player, a VCR, and a microwave. You are financing your car. You have seen seven of the ten top-grossing movies this year. You go to church occasionally, always on Christmas and Easter. You have had three serious relationships, were engaged once, but she left you. While it is true you were a bit of a rabble-rouser in college, you have since settled into a very respectable complacency. You are the epitome of an upright member of society. A very safe man."

"But I . . ." Bill hesitated.

Not a weak man, just strong enough to wonder, to remember a time, a younger time, when he was still . . . thinking. Like deciding to exercise, or read good books again.

"Bill?" Kessler's voice was kind, almost sensuous. "You still with me Bill?"

But Bill wasn't with Mr. Kessler. Bill was ten years back, in a quiet park with an old lover, arguing adamantly about corruption in the government, in the corporate world. . . . *What happened? Age? No. Tired. Maybe I just got tired. A regular paycheck is a nice thing. Decent place to live, a few luxuries (Kessler was right about those.) But this? No. There has to be a middle ground. Or something better.*

"Bill?"

"James." It was more a sigh than a statement. "James, I think you should go." Bill rose to escort him out.

"Why?"

"I'm not like you, James. Or maybe I was, but I don't intend to be any longer. Think about what you're saying, James. 'Organized apathy?' Doesn't something about that sound *wrong* to you?"

"No."

"It does to me. I would like you to leave now, please."

Kessler rose quietly. "I'm sorry, Mr. Blund. We had very high hopes for you. Good day." He walked to the door, opened it, turned back to Bill. "You're going to be sorry, you know. Those who can't swim shouldn't rock the boat."

"The boat is already caught in a hurricane."

Kessler smiled sympathetically as he walked out, quietly closing the door behind him. Standing there in the apartment alone, Bill sensed a power, new or recovered he couldn't tell, but it was there. He felt as if he should thank Kessler for holding up the mirror. Things would be different now.

He walked into the kitchen, poured another cup of coffee.

Tomorrow.

In the hall, James Kessler paused and smiled to himself. It would work. Behind that door something was starting. He wasn't sure exactly what, but it was *something*, and that was a start. Months spent pounding his ideas at people, achieving nothing, had given James the idea. *Good luck, William Blund. Our ranks are growing. Two hundred million minus one.*

The Price of Limes in Managua

A Veri-tale by Susan K. Ito

Manuelito was always the first to spot the foreigners when they pulled into the parking lot. Even with a full hand of cards in his palm he kept one eye trained on the street, watching for that flash of paleness behind the steering wheel. The other boys, laughing and flicking their greasy rags, didn't notice at first when the white Toyota pickup drove up. Then the driver leaned on the horn and the sharp bleating startled them onto their feet. Friendships were dropped at the curb as the boys climbed over each other, elbowing towards the truck, all shouting at once. Manuelito

21

clawed his way through the tangle of bodies, waving his arms.

"I'll watch your truck! I'll guard it for you!" Manuelito screamed in desperation. He tried hard to look smart, to look responsible, to look honest and hard-working. He and the others boys all looked hungry, like they would chew the black rubber off the tires and swallow it down if they could.

The blond-haired, bearded driver stepped out of the pickup, almost slamming one of the smaller boys when he opened the door. "You." He pointed at Manuel. "I'll pay you a million to watch it for a half hour."

Manuelito swiveled his head around, wild with disbelief. He hadn't got picked for weeks. Did that guy really say a million? He thought quickly, how much is a million? Last year a million *cordobas* equaled a dollar. That was a lot. It would take some people a whole day to make that much. But now, especially this week, it probably wasn't worth *mierda*. Enough for a bag of limes though.

"Sure, why not? I'll even clean your headlights. The mirrors too." He shook out the scrap of torn tee-shirt with a flourish.

The other boys were beginning to scatter. One of them muttered bitterly, *"Hijo de puta,* you don't have to show off." Manuelito knew he'd better not gloat. Boys who got picked a lot would be watched, beat up on the way home, all that hard-earned money ripped off. He didn't have any place to keep the money either; he had outgrown his last pair of shoes the month before, and the pockets of his pants opened like empty mouths onto his skinny legs.

He ran around to the other side of the truck and opened the door for the woman. She was tall and pale. The oversized tee-shirt she was wearing bore the faded image of a dove and the words "World Peace." Brown freckles were scattered like muddy raindrops across her skin. Manuelito thought they were the ugliest things he had ever seen. He held his hand back so he wouldn't brush against her. She smiled at him with just the edges of her mouth and let out a little sigh when she looked down at his bony bare feet.

Easing off of the front seat, she asked, "You're going to watch the truck?" He nodded. She pushed a red nylon backpack under the front seat of the vehicle, locked the door, and followed the bearded man across the lot and into the Aeronica airline offices.

The boy knew they would be in there a while. He had looked past the frosted glass door, as it swung back and forth, and had seen people shivering in the air conditioning. They were all holding plastic numbers and were waiting in line to be called. It made him feel good to know that even the *ricos* had to wait in long lines for things, although they did get to sit on vinyl-cushioned seats while they were waiting.

He knew there was a good chance the power would shut down while they were in there. It happened every day. The computers would die with a green blip; the airline agents would throw up their hands and go into the back room to smoke cigarettes. Then, the office would get even hotter than it was outside, a stifling glass box. The clients would sweat and get irritable. There was a rule that if customers left the office, even if the power was out for two hours, they would lose their place in line. It was a perfect business opportunity for Manuel and the other boys. The ones who weren't guarding cars could make some money bringing Cokes to the people waiting in the office. Five million *cordobas* to bring a plastic baggie of soda with a straw in it.

He knelt on the gravel, breathing moisture onto the taillight of the Toyota, rubbing spit into the chrome. He hoped they'd come out right at that moment, that they'd notice the reverence with which he treated the truck, that they'd like it enough to give him an extra tip. When he finished the rear bumper, Manuelito moved forward, carefully polishing each door handle and the trim along the side. He was working on the side mirror when a menacing shape, olive green and black, filled up the reflection. He pretended not to notice, just kept his hand moving on the glass. His stomach shrank up like a balloon, suddenly unknotted. *Luis Arranco.*

Luis Arranco was only sixteen, the same as Manuel's brother Roberto, but he had been with the *contra* for five years, since he was eleven. They said he had killed a lot of people, that he cut off men's hands with a machete, sometimes their ears and tongues, too, and peeled off their eyelids with a pocket knife. He wore those dark glasses all the time, so you couldn't see his eyes, and a green combat jacket over his American-made Jordache blue jeans.

Luis grabbed the rag out of Manuelito's hand, threw it on the ground. He spit on it and growled, "How much that *gringo* give you?"

"A million." Manuelito looked off into the distance, thinking, *Knife . . . where does he keep his knife?*

"Where'd he go?"

He jerked his chin towards the frosted glass doors. "Aeronica."

Luis pressed his face against the window of the truck and leered at the red knapsack on the floor. "Bet they've got a fancy camera in there," he hissed. "I give you a dollar, you little rat, you disappear." The black lenses shone down at him like the dull, hard eyes of an insect.

Luis Arranco flicked the bill under Manuelito's nose, a real greenback. It was grimy and damp, but the boy knew it was worth at least twelve million *cordobas*, probably even fifteen by the next day. He grabbed it and ran across the lot, jumping into the street like a suicide off a bridge. Cars veered around him like repelled magnets, and he emerged, alive, on the other side.

Hysteria pervaded the market that afternoon. People huddled around radios, trying to grasp a shred of meaning about what was to happen the next day. The New Economic Plan, the president called it. A plan that guaranteed that the bills they carried would be worth less than toilet paper by Monday. Men and women waved thick packets of *cordobas*, tied with rubber bands, screaming to trade them for dollars—the dollars that would, as always, rise to the top of the confusion, leaving the people to suffocate among the millions of sorry paper bills that remained.

Manuelito pushed his way through the chaos, clutching the dollar in his fist. He squeezed past a woman in a tight purple dress, her hands a fluttering blur of motion and noise. Four chickens, tied by the feet to her wrists, flapped in desperation, releasing a cloud of feathers. They pecked at each others' heads while the woman shouted at a merchant about the price of onions. Manuelito was almost trampled by a crowd of people, shoving past each other to get to the dairy counter, grabbing for the plastic bags oozing soft white butter. Rounding a corner, he witnessed a collision between a fat merchant hefting sacks of beans and a young girl carrying a big basket of eggs. The eggs shattered at her feet, and she stood in a puddle of slimy yolks, screaming as if each was a murdered child.

Manuelito found Doña Chepita in her stall against the wall. He held up his dollar. "How much for the limes, Chepita? I need a whole bunch."

The older woman narrowed her eyes at him. "Where'd you get that dollar, *m'ijo?*"

He didn't answer. She reached into a wooden crate and started picking out the larger limes.

"I need sugar, too. I know it costs a lot, but I need just a little . . . for Mamá." He wasn't ready to give up the dollar yet, not until he had everything.

She shook her head again and snapped her wrist in a gesture of disgust. *"Ay, qué jodido!* Kids running around like animals on the street, nurses starving themselves to death. How many days now, Manuelito?"

"Eleven days, Doña Chepita. She's feeling . . . better than some of the others. The *limonada* helps. She likes it with sugar. She says it gives her good dreams."

The woman's eyes suddenly grew wet. She wiped them with the back of her hand. "Manuelito, you tell her, if I was still working at the health center, I'd join her in the hunger strike. Maybe when things get better, I'll go back to my nursing job. . . ." She looked over the boy's head and her voice cracked. She blinked her eyes.

"Listen, *m'ijo,* you keep that greenback. It's going to be worth a lot more tomorrow. You give your mamá *un abrazo fuerte* from her *compañera* Chepita, okay?" She filled a small bag with sugar and tied it with a piece of white string that she broke off with her teeth. She placed the bag carefully on top of the limes that he balanced against his chest.

Manuelito looked at the woman, sitting among the broken wooden fruit crates, at her skinny, dirty feet in their rubber sandals. He remembered visiting Chepita and his mother at the health center. In their white uniforms they had looked like angels. He had trailed them through the neighborhoods, as they knocked on doors, offering vaccinations, vitamins, and comic books about breastfeeding and measles. He remembered the classes that Chepita used to give to pregnant women, drawing pictures on the blackboard of upside-down babies, the way she would shake her finger at them in mock sternness, how they would laugh and pat their bellies. Then, he thought of his mother, lying on a mattress at the Red Cross, her face growing thinner every day, the hollows deepening under her eyes.

"Maybe Mamá should have bought one of those popsicle carts, Chepita," he murmured. "Maybe she should set up a place here next to you . . ."

"No, Manuelito! No!" She answered in a voice that was tight as a wire. "Your mother is fighting for something. God knows if it's going to make any difference. This government could let them all die before giving an inch. But she's fighting."

His face froze, the words like hard little pebbles in his mouth. "Do you think she's going to die?"

"Not your mamá. She's a tough one. Now go, get out of here, take these to her! Make her a sweet *limonada.* She'll like that. And don't forget, you tell her I'm with her." Chepita pulled him close, as if to embrace him, then swatted him on the rump. The boy hugged the green fruit to his shirt, the bag of sugar tucked under his chin, and snaked his way through the market crowd without dropping one lime.

The sun glared down unmercifully. Manuelito danced to keep his calluses from melting on the pavement. Each time he licked his lips there was less to wet them with. The limes were warm and soft in his hands. He fought the desire to rip one open with his teeth, to taste the bitter green juice in his mouth. Only five more blocks.

At last, in the distance he could see the Red Cross sign, hanging over the sidewalk. He took off his shirt, tying the fruit and the bag of sugar carefully into the center. Once they were secure, he broke into a run, swinging the bundle over his head.

In front of the building a large white sheet had been tied to the entrance; stenciled in red paint, the familiar words: THE HUNGER STRIKERS ASK FOR ONLY ONE NOURISHMENT: SOLIDARITY. As he approached the metal gate at the open side of the building, he could see the strikers, doctors and nurses in white uniforms and green surgical outfits. They had risen from the mats on the floor and were shaking hands with a group of visitors. His mother stood with them, wobbling slightly on her bird legs. Manuelito rushed towards her to offer his gift. Suddenly, he stopped still, the blood throbbing in his ears. Speaking with his mother were the bearded *gringo,* whose white truck he had abandoned, and the freckled woman. They embraced her, patting her thin shoulder, then turned to leave.

Manuel's stomach cramped; he ducked his head so she wouldn't recognize him. But his mother saw him and called out, "Here comes my son. Manuelito, come here!" A smile lighted her haggard face as she reached out her hand to him.

There was no choice but to go to her, holding the shirt bulging with fruit. "Here, Mamá," he mumbled. "I'm going to make you a *limonada.*"

His mother hugged him to her, stroking his head. Her words buzzed around him. *"M'ijo . . . such a big help."*

The *gringa* woman looked down at his face. For a moment her blue eyes flashed with anger. Then she turned to Manuel's mother and smiled. "I'm sure he's a good son."

Cringing, his face on fire, Manuelito slipped from his mother's embrace and scurried out of the large room. He darted through a narrow corridor, pausing briefly to grab a plastic bucket, then hurried into a tiny washroom. His hands shaking, he lifted the bucket to the tap and filled it. He peeled back the rippled skin from the first lime, then squeezed its juice, like blood, into the water.

Pearl,
Shadow and Light

A Veri-tale by John D. Nesbitt

That first summer we were married she cut off her hair, had it cut off a little at a time. We were broke, living in a basement apartment, and she found it depressing. So she cut off her hair and tried to get pregnant.

"It's okay," I said. "Get your hair cut the way you want. If you don't like the way it looks, you can let it grow back."

"I feel like a miserable mole, living down in this hole," she would say. Then we would make love and she would tell me, crying, "What I want most of all, more than anything, is to have your baby."

Words like that made me feel better, even if we weren't set up for baby. I had just gone back to work, and we were more or less agreed that we would do house, baby, and car, in that order. Now, she was pushing baby first, maybe both house and baby at once, I wasn't sure. But if it made her happy, I could adjust. And it was exciting to try for baby.

Some of it was my fault, in a way—the part about not having a better place to live. The summer before, when we were engaged, I was living in the mobile home. One Saturday afternoon she drove out to see me while I was working in the yard, transplanting some young shade trees to what was to be the back yard. We sat in the shade of the mobile home and drank beer, cold bottled beer, in the warm shade. I set the water running slowly to soak the trees in their new places, and I thought about the holes I would have to go back and fill in where I had dug up the trees in the windbreak.

She was thinking about the mobile home. "What's going to become of this thing?"

"Oh, I think we could live in it for a while, until we get the house built."

"And where does the house go?"

She already knew. I had told her more than once. I still harbored the plan I had started with Stephanie—to build an earth-sheltered home down the hill a ways. It was what anyone would want, a southern exposure and out of the wind, somewhat.

So I said, "Down over there."

And she said, "No, I don't want to live in the ground. I want the house here."

"Right here?"

"Right here. Where this thing is."

"What kind of a house, then?"

"A regular house. A *normal* house."

I looked at the little trees and then said, pointing with my thumb, "Then I take it you don't want to live in this thing." She knew, because I had told her, that two people could live in it.

"If you don't get rid of it, I won't marry you." Those were her words as we sat in the warm shade, drinking cold beer, on that Saturday afternoon.

Looking back, I could ask, what drove me to it? Why would I find myself, months later, as the wind blew and the snowflakes fell, helping strangers rip out the skirting, cut the roots of water supply and sewer hook-up, take down the fence, and jockey that long, awkward crate off my property and on down the road? Partly, it was because I wanted to get along. I was living in the shadow of failure from my first marriage, and I didn't want to hear again that I was too hard to get along with.

Partly, it was because she had already set the pattern, earlier, that she would have things as she wanted. After we had been going out for a couple of months, she decided we should just be friends—meaning, we wouldn't sleep together anymore. Then, a month and a half later, she decided we could be lovers again. I was thrilled. In another three months I was engaged. Looking back, I think that pattern set me up for getting rid of the mobile home, even though at the time I imagined I was trying not to be too hard to get along with. So I overdid it the other way and made it too easy for her to get her way.

I got rid of the trailer, took an apartment in town, got married as planned, got laid off in the dead of winter, and ended up living in a hole in the ground anyway.

It was dark and cool down in the basement, so we could go to bed early on those summer evenings. The awareness of baby was a dimension I hadn't known before, something that had never come around with

Stephanie. Even if I wasn't quite ready for it in my own sense of order, it was a strong pull. "I want to have your baby." The words of my Indian princess.

Even with her long black hair cut off, she was the dark earth to me—child of the earth, and earth itself. I wasn't just making love with my wife. I was mingling with all of it: ravens, horses, juniper trees, clear water, desert sun. Her adoptive parents vanished, and she was the Indian princess, anonymous, without personal connections or attachments. Child of the earth, orphan—wild dark fruit by nature, pale Hoosier by nurture. When we tried for baby, the midwesterners were gone from the picture.

Thinking of the children that would be, I imagined them with her features—quick, dark eyes, aquiline nose, thick, rich hair. Smart kids, like their mother, they would also have the spirit, the straight line back to the desert. The heat and the strength of the ancient sun would flow in their blood. That was my picture.

I think some of her depression came from the change in hormones from going off the pill, and I think some of it came from baby's failure to become. Some of it came, no doubt, simply because things weren't going her way. I thought she might cheer up if she got a job; we could certainly use the money.

"I'm not going back to waiting tables," she said. "My parents didn't put me through college for that."

"It's okay," I said. "We're getting by." We were.

After work I would go out to the place, usually by myself, and take care of the horse and the plant life. Several months after the trailer was gone, a friend brought out his tractor and helped me root out the cement footings, so there was a long, bare depression, surrounded by new trees, lilac bushes, lawn, and flower beds. It was a bit odd by some standards, to have a hole right in the middle of a well-kept yard, but it was a pretty place that summer. We set a little campfire pit in the low spot, and we had a couple of picnics there. We also camped, one weekend.

We were sitting by the campfire, appreciating out loud the simplicity of it all, having fun with the idea that I was a ten percent cowboy and she was half Indian. Eventually, we got to the point where I held my hand in front of my face, palm inward, separated my fingers two-and-two into a vee, squinted through, and claimed, "I could find you in the dark."

She stuck out her tongue and winked in the firelight. "You're just a pony soldier. You're no scout."

The upshot of it was that she went into the tent and came out wrapped in only a blanket, a cotton serape we used for a bed cover. I would have ten minutes, with my eyes closed, to find her. She was free to move around, but both of us would stay on all fours. She claimed to have a better sense of time than I did, so she would tell me when the game was up.

I started from a corner, imagined a diagonal across the lawn, and decided to cut the field in half, zig-zagging back and forth from my course. If that failed, I would try a circle.

The direct method did fail, so when I felt the lilac bushes poking at my forehead, I started the circle to my left. It was probably a bad circle, but I had a method in mind. I crawled along, trying to keep my ears and nose open. My original joke was that I could sniff her out in the dark, but she had taken off her smoky clothes, so I had to listen for the whisper of the blanket on the grass.

After a little while I heard it, and then again. I scrambled, turned, scrambled, and lunged—and caught the fringe of the serape. Then I came to her, hand over hand, crawling, with my eyes still closed, finding and confirming, then conforming, mingling with her softness as the campfire crackled in the background.

"May I open my eyes now?"

"Go ahead."

"How did I do?"

"Not bad for a pony soldier."

Still, no baby, through that summer and into the fall. She counseled with her mother, conferred with the baby doctor. She continued to hate the basement, and I wondered why this child of the earth would be so set against it, unless the earth had been nurtured out of her. Then I made it into a question of nature; I imagined her as the sun princess, rebelling against her confinement.

This princess business was a child of my own imagination, which I clung to long after I had any cause. It came from the story as it came to me from her, as it had come to her. Her mother was Indian, Papago. Her father, unknown, was Anglo. The mother had died and left the baby alone in the world. A kindly couple, who had raised two boys but had always wanted a girl, adopted her. And here she was now, a grown woman, beautiful, a study in heredity and environment.

This kindly couple, although I call them the Hoosiers, are from Iowa. I could call them corn gentry, but they aren't farmers, never were. So I just call them Hoosiers—stereotypical mid-western, middle-class palefaces, right down to the four television sets, three cars, and unacknowledged gay son. I am a paleface too, but I don't lie about my family, so I have found my way to describe that difference. Deep down, I'm still bitter about the way they raised the child in a bubble of dishonesty, and I try to make light of it by calling them something they aren't. It's my idea of a joke, I suppose, and maybe not a very good one, since they didn't even have to come from the midwest to be in the bubble manufacturing business.

At about the time I was adjusting to the idea of yanking out the mobile home, my princess was fresh out of college and back home, living with mom and dad. Also living with them was mom's youngest brother, Len. He did a little yard work, a little scraping and painting on the house trim; he helped with the kitchen work and watched soap operas with his sister. Mom took care of him because he was her baby brother and because he was just getting by on disability checks for a bad back. He was also trying to stay sober, and doing a pretty good job of it, too.

Along about the middle of the summer, mom and dad and daughter went on a visit back home, to Davenport, Iowa. They left Uncle Len to keep an eye on the house, and me to keep an eye on him.

"He's doing so well," she said. It sounded like her mom, who had probably said it first.

He must have started drinking right after they left. By the time I checked with him the next day, he was on a bender. There was a bottle of vodka on the coffee table, a large triangular glazed ashtray full of stubs, and two crumpled cigarette packs. He offered me one of dad's economy-brand beers, and I accepted.

I had barely gotten started on my beer when he up and told me he was her father. Just like that.

"What do you mean?"

"I'm her father. Jim and Barbara adopted her from inside the family."

"Oh, shit. And she doesn't know?"

"No, and no one outside the family knows, either."

"Except me."

"Except you."

"Why did you tell me? That's quite a bomb to lay on me."

"You love her, don't you?"

"Of course I do."

"Well, I thought you should know. And, since you love her, I thought you'd accept it."

It wasn't until weeks later, after Len had gone down the road, that I figured out his real motive—to pressure mom and dad into bringing out the truth before the wedding. I think he wanted an end to the long masquerade he had been drawn into, but he didn't have the nerve to do the unveiling himself. So he rigged it. He told me, he told his sister he told me, and then he left. He was a Hoosier, too.

In the course of that afternoon, that strange afternoon in the stale, curtained living room, he told me assorted stories and facts, while I drank half a dozen of those cheap beers. The mother was still alive. She was a drunk, just as he was. There were brothers and sisters scattered all over, from his other marriage, her other marriage, and their time together. Three others had been adopted, outside the family. A sister was dead, a brother was in prison. Len showed me a scar on his stomach that, according to his story, came from a fight in Oklahoma. They buried the other man, and they put Len in prison for a few years. That was between marriages.

So here I was, engaged to be married, trying to sell my mobile home, sitting on a twenty-three-year-old family secret, and wondering when it was going to break. While I wondered, I came to understand how such a secret kept on going. Part of it was to protect little brother, and part of it was to shield the baby from the truth that was all around her. Once mom and dad committed themselves to the lie, they kept it up, covering the truth with layer after layer of pampering. They spoiled her rotten, gave her everything she wanted, so that if and when the truth ever broke, they could say, as they did, "We did it because we loved you."

In the meanwhile, she learned that when she put her pretty little foot down, she got away with it. It was a strange pattern, to pamper a baby and nurture a tyrant. And I had become part of the pattern long before I realized it.

It was an ugly scene, as she recounted it to me, that day the truth came to light. It is a small part in this story about the search for baby, but it was a major event in my wife's life. After she had been ravaged by the truth and had thrown a pretty dark fit in return, she came to see me. We were in the process of ordering wedding invitations. It was one of the last evenings I spent in the trailer; the weather was cold and wet and bleak, as we sat on the little sofa in the living room. I hugged her and patted her beautiful black hair as she choked out the story. Really, there were two stories together—the trauma of that afternoon, and the secret of long ago. Most of the latter I had already heard, and now we put our versions together.

"Did he tell you what my name was before I was adopted?"

"No. What was it?"

"Pearl. My name was Pearl."

I had mixed feelings in all of this. On one hand I despised the Hoosiers for their lying and their over-protectiveness. I thought they should have let her grow more naturally into what she would be. It seemed to me that they had spoiled the child of the earth, shaped her into a stupid clay pot, and yet I knew, at the same time, that the orphan princess was a form of my own devising, and she was half Hoosier after all.

As I say, I hung onto this picture for a longer time than was called for—on through the first year of marriage and all our struggles to find baby. It was still with me when spring came a second time upon our bare parcel of land. One afternoon in May, I was moving those same little shade trees again, after their two-year stay, to make room for the house we would build and then fight over. I was down in the hole, wrapping burlap around the ball of dirt and roots, when she drove up. I wrestled the tree out of the earth and laid it, horizontally, on the ground.

"Congratulations," she said. "You're going to be a daddy."

Cautious optimism, to say the least. Through all our troubles in bringing baby together, we had learned that my wife's reproductive system was imperfectly developed, probably as the result of her own mother's drinking during pregnancy. This imperfect system, we understood, could bring grief at any point along the way.

By now I was used to being uncertain about how I ought to feel. Through one crisis after another we focused on her feelings and more or less set mine aside. Now, there was a promise of baby. I was supposed to be happy, but there was such a cloud over

46

us that I couldn't let myself go. It was a good thing I didn't, because when the miscarriage came, I didn't have so far to fall. Instead of grief-stricken, I was only numb—numb, I guess, from the pillar-to-post series of events I had been through.

It's not really a blur, that episode. It's a sequence of dull, painful pictures: my wife, pale and terrified; the pastor, explaining that God's way is mysterious; the doctor, assuring us it would turn out all right; her mother, smoking one cigarette after another; then my wife, full of anger and no clear direction to send it, full of grief without a clear object to grieve.

She took it plenty bad. She had really wanted the baby, and now it was lost, a broken promise. None of it made sense.

After a short stay at the hospital she laid up at her parents' house, where I visited her four times a day. It was an unusual arrangement to me, but it was the way she wanted it. On one of my visits she bitched at me for being late. I shrugged and got up to get a cup of coffee in the kitchen. Mom followed me, and as I stirred the cream into the coffee she said, "Be patient with her. Tammy just needs more love."

The doctors told us we could try again, and when the house was built, we did. But something had changed. As I imagined our future children, they no longer looked like quick, dark warriors. They began to look like Hoosiers. Something changed in her, too. I heard it. At some point she had left off saying "your baby" and "our baby." It became "a baby," and later on it was "No baby."

Not ever. Not by birth. Not by adoption. "I just can't do it," she said.

There was more to this than I can claim to understand. I tried to set myself aside, as it seemed I had been doing for a long time, and grasp how the trauma of miscarriage and the disillusionment of her adoption had closed two doors in her mind. Then, to make sense for myself, I had to see it in terms of what it meant to me. She was getting her way. She was putting her foot down.

"Maybe you'll think differently after a little time has passed. This doesn't have to be a snap decision."

"It's not a snap decision. I've thought about it and thought about it, and I know what I want." We were sitting on the couch in our new living room, and she put her head against my chest. "I just can't, that's all." Then she cried, and I held her tight and stroked her beautiful hair. It was growing back. She moved her head to speak. "Is it all right with you?"

"Of course it's all right with me. Both of those decisions have to start with you." I patted her hair.

"We're going to be all right, aren't we?"

"Yes," I said, "we're going to be all right," but as I said it, I had the strange new feeling that I was lying. I knew I was trying not to be hard to get along with. But I was getting an idea of what it meant when her mom said she needed more love.

"You know I need someone to take care of me."

"Yes, and you know I've wanted to." I was beginning to realize, that evening as we sat on the sofa, that there would be a child anyway, this child that I held, this child that had been handed from one set of parents to another and then to me. I had hoped that with baby she would grow out of her selfishness and join me as a parent. But she was determined to remain the child, and it was not the child I had grown to look for. My eyes had been opened. That's why I was being so easy to get along with. I knew I needed to find some way out of being a childless parent . . . or worse, my child's lover.

One of our wedding gifts had been a stoneware vase, something vaguely Indian or Southwestern, I guess. It was in dull earth tones, with a body the shape of a tulip bulb and a neck too narrow to put any reasonable number of flowers in. But it was pleasing to the eye. One day, after we had moved into the house, we found the vase where it had fallen from the oak buffet and broken to pieces. Neither of us had been home all day, and no pets had been inside. As nearly as we could tell, the vase had simply fallen and broken. Maybe vibration from the railroad tracks or from the constant wind had brought it to the edge.

They spoiled her and I failed her, that's how I see it. I had my own mystique to fit onto her, and when that was way gone, as gone as the vase, I gave up on her. I had become her parent, when I thought I was her protecting lover, and now that I saw where I was, I didn't want to be there.

Pearl went on to an older man, much older than myself, a man whose kids were already raised. He was her counselor first, and now he takes care of her. As for myself, I sit in the shade of a tree now big enough to reciprocate. I see the diamond and emerald sparkle of the newly watered lawn. In my mind I picture children, frolicking there, and at my side, a woman.

Elevator Up

A Veri-tale by Janet Schumer

From the very beginning he felt there was something wrong. The interviewer at the employment agency had given him this address in midtown Manhattan, and the listing of the offices located in the building definitely said the fifty-fourth floor. Yet there appeared to be no elevator service to that floor.

Walter Hewlitt looked down the two aisles of busy elevators a second time: Local to 18, Express 19 to 35, Express 36 to 53. He checked the registry again. Atlas Company, Floor 54. He looked more closely. This time he noticed an arrow under the listing, directing him away from the crowded lobby and the rows of elevators, down a quiet back corridor. There stood a solitary elevator marked "Floor 54 only." The elevator was waiting. He was perplexed to find the only elevator to that floor set apart from those in the busy lobby. And, unlike the others, which were attended by young men in bright uniforms, this one was self-service.

He pressed the button marked *Up*. As the elevator made its noiseless climb, he examined himself in the mirror—a balding man in his mid-fifties, of average height, and carrying a little too much weight around the middle. He cleared his throat apprehensively. It was inconceivable, after working all those years at the Necker Machinery Company, that Necker Machinery was in receivership and he was starting a new job. A man should have some security against such eventualities, he thought bitterly.

The elevator door glided open. He found himself in an enormous, brightly-lit office.

"Mr. Hewlitt, we have been expecting you." A white-haired man sitting near the elevator door rose and extended his hand. "I am Gregory Bowers. Welcome to the Atlas Company."

"How do you do," Mr. Hewlitt murmured, clearing his throat. "The agency said I was to see a Mr. Atlas."

"Yes, of course. But not just now. If the agency sent you, you are acceptable to him. Mr. Atlas sees no new employee until he has been here about a week. He likes to give our new men time to get adjusted." Bowers led him into the room. "Let me show you where you will be working. We have an urgent need for experienced men in your age group—scientists, engineers, and mathematicians. We want you to get started right away."

"I was beginning to think my age was a handicap in finding a new job," Walter Hewlitt admitted.

"Not here," answered Bowers.

Mr. Hewlitt followed his guide past rows and rows of desks, set out methodically, like a field of cabbage. Behind the desks he noticed men working intently, all of them middle-aged. He rather expected to be introduced to some of them, but Bowers led him straight across the room. None of the men showed any curiosity or friendliness; none of them glanced up as he passed.

He found himself at a desk next to a glass wall, with a staggering view of the street fifty-four stories down. The drop to the street was too close to his chair for him to feel comfortable.

"There is a world of security in this glass wall," Bowers assured him. "If you have any questions, ask me. We do not encourage conversation between the employees during working hours." He left on the clean desk a manila folder, containing a number of personnel forms and an outline of a mathematical project to be computed.

Walter's methodical mind applauded such efficiency. He filled out the personnel forms and then studied his instructions. They involved principles with which he was familiar, and he understood exactly what to do. Even though he was not informed of the over-all project on which he was employed, his work would not present any special difficulty. He worked happily all morning, challenged by new problems and fascinated, as always, by figures.

At twelve o'clock Mr. Bowers approached his desk. "Mr. Hewlitt, your lunch hour is between noon and one o'clock. If you are ready to leave now, the elevator is waiting."

Mr. Hewlitt rose and looked about in astonishment. On each desk was a neat paper bag; each man was quietly eating his lunch. He smiled inwardly, wondering whether they all had ulcers or were simply saving lunch money. In any event, he thought with amusement, the office had the appearance of a roomful of robots.

He shared the elevator with a heavy-set man, whose thick red hair was tinged with gray.

"I'm Ben Buckley," he said, offering his hand. "How about joining me for lunch?"

"Fine." Walter introduced himself.

"That quiet office is too much for me. Let's eat in a noisy restaurant," Ben suggested.

Over their first course Ben confided, "Now, I feel more human. There's something wrong with that set-up, Hewlitt. What do you think of the place?"

"It seems all right to me. It's very modern, very efficient."

"No, Hewlitt. I've been there three days, and I tell you, something is definitely wrong. First of all, you were hired through an agency without an interview, right?"

"Yes. Nothing wrong with that." Walter was feeling a bit defensive.

"They offered you an extremely high salary, right? More than you had been earning, and more than you would have asked for?"

"Yes."

"And have you noticed that there are no young men there? Everyone is at least fifty or over."

Hewlitt agreed. "That's understandable. Mr. Bowers said they wanted men with experience, men who have worked in their field for many years. A younger man doesn't have that experience."

Buckley leaned across the table and lowered his voice.

"Haven't you noticed that the men are all odd birds? Have you ever been in any other office where no one talks to anyone else? No conversation of any kind. No one gets up from his desk for a glass of water or to go to the washroom. They do nothing but work. I haven't seen one person lift his head up from his desk all morning. Watch them this afternoon. There must be at least two hundred men in that room. No one talks. No one walks around. It's peculiar."

Still, Hewlitt stood his ground. "They're probably too busy. They're so busy they don't even go out for lunch."

"No, there's some other explanation. And how about that elevator?"

"What about it?"

"There are only two buttons—*Up* and *Down*. You can't stop on any other floor. Incidentally, Walter, have you tried to take a regular elevator to the fifty-fourth floor?"

"No, I haven't," Hewlitt replied.

"Well, I've tried. They say the fifty-third is the top floor. I've gotten out on the fifty-third floor and looked for a stairway up the extra flight. There is none. There's a stairway down, but none up. As far as the rest of the building is concerned, there is no fifty-fourth floor. The whole thing gives me an uneasy feeling."

"There must be some logical explanation," Walter insisted.

"What is logic?" Ben asked.

Walter thought a moment. "It's a science which proves the reason and validity of a thought."

"No," said Ben. "It can also be a device which convinces us and makes argument useless."

The afternoon passed rapidly for Walter Hewlitt. He loved working with figures. He could get so involved with a problem that he became oblivious of the hour and time made no impression on him. He could understand the complete absorption of the other men in the office. Ben appeared to be a pleasant-enough fellow, with perhaps a little too much imagination. In the world of figures and facts there is no need for imagination.

At five o'clock that afternoon he was startled by the sound of the scraping of many chairs. As if by some prearranged signal, all the men arose as of one body and filed to the single elevator. They lined up, awaiting their turn to descend. Ten entered at each time, and the line shortened rapidly.

Walter joined Ben in line, and they entered the elevator together.

"Did you notice it?" Ben asked.

"Notice what?"

"None of the others would step into the elevator with us. Until you came today, I've always been in here alone." The elevator made its noiseless descent to the ground floor. As they parted, Ben was still musing to himself, "I wonder what makes them act so peculiar?"

Walter ordinarily would have been in no hurry to get home. Since he had lost his wife eighteen months ago, there would be no one at home to greet him, no welcoming kiss, no aroma of dinner being cooked. It had been a happy marriage, and he was devastated when she died. Lately, however, he recognized that he was coming to terms with his grief. His memory of his wife and their years together seemed to give him a melancholy pleasure.

Tonight the strangeness of his new job made him anxious to return to the comfort of everything familiar at home. The cleaning woman had left the apartment clean and smelling faintly of furniture polish. He walked across the deep-piled carpet in his living room, past the dining room with its polished furniture, and into the kitchen. There he removed his jacket and made himself a cold supper.

The second day there was another manila folder waiting on Walter's desk. He examined the new problem. His instructions were clear enough, but today he felt he was a bit beyond his depth. He wondered what it was that he was computing. Whatever it was, it seemed foreign to anything he had ever encountered. His head started to pound and his collar felt too tight. *This damn problem is giving me a migraine headache,* he thought. *I need air.* He leaned over to the window and tried to open it. It would not budge. He put all his strength into the next effort. It would not lift. He felt foolish, although he realized no one was watching him. Loosening his collar, he walked over to Mr. Bower's desk.

"Is there something wrong with the windows?" Walter asked.

"They are locked."

"Why?"

"The air in the office is regulated," Bowers answered patiently. "It is air-conditioned in the warm weather, heated in the cold weather. It is also dehumidified and slightly pressurized. It is always the same temperature and the same pressure throughout the year. Tests prove that men work at their peak of efficiency under proper atmospheric conditions. The air outside is imperfect. In here it is always the same."

"Who has the key?"

"Mr. Atlas."

Walter remembered something else he wanted to ask.

"Mr. Bowers, could you tell me about the project I'm working on?"

"Mr. Atlas will advise you at the proper time."

Feeling slightly abashed, Walter returned slowly to his desk. It was almost lunch-time. He could wait until noon to get some fresh air.

He and Ben Buckley again shared the elevator, and once out on the street, he felt better. Over lunch Walter told Ben of his experience.

"I thought I would suffocate," he said.

"I felt peculiar on my second day, too," Ben admitted.

The men ate in companionable silence for a while. Then Ben spoke.

"By the way, Hewlitt, do you smoke?"

"No. I had a bad fright a number of years ago. I resolved then to give up smoking."

"What happened?"

"My family was camping down at Kingsbury State Beach. One afternoon I swam quite a ways out into the ocean, and I ran completely out of energy. I didn't think I'd make it back to shore. Trying to move my arms and legs was a tremendous effort. I was gasping for breath—thought my lungs would burst. I haven't had a cigarette since then. Why do you ask?"

"Well, because that's another strange thing about the Atlas Company: In that entire office I'm the only smoker. The only ash tray in that whole barn of a place is on my desk. I go through three packs a day. I can't believe that among all those men I'm the only one who smokes."

"A lot of offices today have a no smoking policy."

"I don't think it's a 'policy.' Nobody's said anything to me about not smoking," Ben insisted. "They just don't smoke. And another thing. Have you met the boss yet—Mr. Atlas?"

"Not yet. Have you?"

"I meet him tomorrow. Another peculiar character. Waits about a week before he meets a new employee and keeps himself in hiding. Frankly, if I could get another job, I'd take it—at half the pay. But who else would hire a statistician who's fifty-five years old?" Ben hesitated, then backtracked. "No, not at half the pay. I have two sons in college. Brilliant boys. It takes a lot of money to put those two through college at the same time. I'll stick it out for their sake." He paused for a second, then added, "I shouldn't complain. They're worth any sacrifice."

"I have a married daughter and one grandson." Walter volunteered.

That evening Walter tried to put through a telephone call to his daughter and son-in-law, who now lived in Oregon. First, the circuits were busy. When he finally reached their number, he got the babysitter, who explained that everyone was out and his grandson was napping. As Walter hung up the phone, he realized that something else was missing from that strange office. There were no telephones on any of the desks.

The next day at lunch Walter found Ben extremely agitated. He had three martinis with his half-eaten meal.

"This afternoon I go in to see Mr. Atlas," Ben explained, inhaling deeply from his cigarette. "I tell you, this set-up is all wrong. I'm afraid. If I didn't need the money, I'd walk out right now."

"The place is a little unusual, but nothing worth worrying about," Walter assured him.

A few hours later Mr. Bowers escorted Ben Buckley through the massive door marked "Private" at the front of the room. He was still in there at five o'clock, when Walter left.

At home, after a light supper, Walter spent a long time trying to analyze his feeling that there might be something unusual about this whole project. He thought about Ben and his doubts. It was a long time before he fell asleep; when he finally did, he dreamt that Mr. Atlas was nine feet tall.

The next morning it was raining. Walter's rubbers sloshed through the wet corridor near the busy elevators. Puddles from dripping umbrellas shone on the floor. He walked down the side corridor to the solitary elevator to his floor. There the corridor was clean and dry. Over a hundred men must have passed this way before him, yet even the elevator floor was dry. There was no indication that anyone had used it. As the elevator ascended, Walter examined himself in the mirror. He looked as though he could use more sleep.

He walked through the maze of desks, anxious to hear what Ben had to tell him. The moment he saw Ben's face, he stopped stock still. Ben's reddish complexion was ashen gray, and like the others, he was bent over his work in utter concentration. Missing from the top of his desk was the overflowing ash tray.

Hewlitt walked quietly to his own desk. The office seemed unnaturally silent. He could almost hear his own breathing. As he opened the new manila envelope which was waiting for him on his desk, even the project he was working on seemed mysterious and sinister.

During the morning he cast surreptitious glances in Ben's direction and noticed that he was not smoking. Nor was he moving about in his usual restless, impatient manner.

At lunch-time Walter waited for him—until he noticed, sitting on Ben's desk, a neat brown paper bag. After lunch Walter decided to speak to him. As he approached, Ben was already absorbed in the papers on his desk.

"Ben, I was wondering . . . " The red-haired man looked up. A complete stranger. There was no sign of interest or recognition in the glazed eyes. The face was set in a slight frown. It was uncanny. Ben looked so much like the others that Walter wondered with horror if he would even recognize him again. He stumbled back to his own desk as in a nightmare.

The rain closed out any view from the windows. Only the bright fluorescent lights were reflected. He had the impression that they were in a sealed vacuum, floating above the earth, unconnected to the building, unrooted in reality. The office was so silent that it seemed as though he were alone.

"Mr. Atlas will see you now." Walter came back to reality with a jolt. Mr. Bowers was standing next to him.

"Now? But my week is not up yet," Hewlitt objected.

"Mr. Atlas is ready to see you today."

Bowers led the way to the front of the large room, Walter following stiffly, clearing his throat. He straightened his lapels and patted his hair.

Mr. Bowers opened the massive door.

"Mr. Atlas, Mr. Walter Hewlitt. Mr. Hewlitt, may I present Mr. Atlas." And Mr. Bowers left him. Walter found himself in a large square room, two walls of which were windows from floor to ceiling. The room was devoid of any furniture with the exception of a leather chair, a long desk, and a water cooler.

Mr. Atlas was neither tall nor short, neither dark nor light, neither young nor old. He had no distinguishing features. His face was the type one might see many times without remembering it. He stood, and indicated that Walter be seated in the leather chair.

When Mr. Atlas spoke, however, his physical blandness was forgotten. His voice was vital, deep, authoritative. Walter had the feeling that he had heard that voice before.

"Mr. Hewlitt, I have been watching you. I like the way you work. I feel we are going to have a mutually satisfactory relationship."

"Thank you, sir."

"Please pardon me for waiting so long before meeting you. I like to know what a man can do before we sit down together." His manner was charming. "I am very satisfied with you."

"That is good to hear. You know, I've been wondering, what kind of work does the company do?"

"We will get to that before our little talk is over. There also must be other questions on your mind, which we will discuss. Let me just say now that we are working on a big project, and we need every available brain we can get. We are using only men who have passed their fiftieth birthday." He paused. The silence made Walter uncomfortable. He was relieved when Mr. Atlas continued. "Let me tell you why we selected you. You are fifty-three years old. Widower. You have one daughter, whom you see only a few times a year."

Hewlitt nodded.

"You have been employed by one concern during all of your working years, and now they are out of business. Necker Machinery represented a kind of security, which you found most important. You felt your world had crumbled when you lost that job."

How does he know all of this?

"You do not like change. You have been lonesome since your wife died."

"Just a moment, Mr. Atlas. My personal life is not important here. Let's keep this conversation on a business level."

"This is all very pertinent," Atlas insisted.

Hewlitt remained silent.

"There is still more that we know about you. You are afraid to make decisions. You are not aggressive. You were pleased when you came here and found only men in your own age group. You do not want to compete with younger men."

Atlas walked over to the water cooler. He filled a glass and placed it on his desk.

"You feel life has nothing more to offer you. Sometimes you feel like a man old before your time."

Hewlitt started to speak, but Atlas silenced him with a cold stare. His voice went on, smooth and convincing.

"This is our proposition, Hewlitt: We need you. No one else can say this to you. Not even your daughter. She has her own family, her own life now. We need your brain.

"And now I will tell you why we are using men who have passed their fiftieth birthday." Mr. Atlas spoke slowly, emphasizing each word. "We enter into a contract with you. We offer you complete security. We guarantee perfect health for as long as you live. We protect you against everything that can hurt you, anger you, or upset you. In exchange for this guarantee, we want your brain free from any disturbing thought or emotion that might interfere with your work. Your body will be an instrument for your brain and will be kept in perfect condition. Your pleasure will be in your work. You will be happy here. You have seen how our men work, in complete absorption. Nothing distracts them. They are doing what they enjoy."

"What happens when they go home?"

"They go through the regular routines to which they have accustomed themselves. But now they have a protective shell about them. They never become sick

71

or tired. They never worry. Nothing bothers them. They cannot feel pain." Mr. Atlas hesitated, then remarked craftily. "You will never have another migraine headache."

He had touched a sensitive chord.

"It is quite a temptation," Hewlitt conceded. *Why did this voice seem familiar?*

"We will make your decisions," Atlas continued. His voice filled the room like the sound of the ocean surf, shutting out all other sounds. "We take over your personal worries. You will have complete peace of mind. All we want is your trained, undisturbed brain, working for us."

"And the work I'll be doing?"

"The kind of work you have done this week—what you have been trained to do."

"I enjoy the work. I find it stimulating."

Atlas's voice flowed smoothly on. "You will draw your salary as long as you live." He paused. "And, starting tomorrow, it will be doubled."

"Doubled?" Hewlitt was incredulous.

"You will receive more money than you ever thought you would earn. Remember, also, you will have perfect health for the rest of your life."

"How can you guarantee perfect health?" Hewlitt asked.

Atlas picked up the glass from his desk. "It is very simple," he said. "One can do whatever one sets his mind on doing. There is no limitation to the power of the mind. This is our contract. A drink from my water cooler will seal our agreement."

Atlas handed him the glass. Their fingers brushed. Atlas's cold hand felt bloodless.

"Drink it now," Atlas insisted. "A toast to your future."

Hewlitt looked at the glass and the seemingly harmless transparent liquid.

Atlas repeated, hypnotically. "Drink it. Your throat is dry. No more pain. You will never know sorrow or worry. We take all these from you."

Hewlitt tore his eyes away and looked out the windows. It was still raining.

Atlas's voice was persuasive, insistent. "You will never have to make another decision. Let me make this one for you. Drink from the glass. You are thirsty. You need a drink. It tastes good."

Think, Hewlitt said to himself. *Is this what I really want? It sounds so appealing. But no pain means also no pleasure. If nothing could hurt me, neither could anything make me happy. Have years of living made me weak?*

Atlas was speaking again. "Drink from the glass. It takes just a moment . . . "

"It takes just a moment." No wonder the voice was familiar. In that agonizing swim to shore, he had heard a deep, surging voice, talking to him. Perhaps it was the pounding in his head or the motion of the waves, but it seemed to be saying, "Relax, relax. Oblivion takes just a moment."

"No," Hewlitt said, rising. "This is not for me."

"One moment, Hewlitt. I will not force you. That is not our way. But do not turn away from the highest measure of security."

"You are not offering me security," Hewlitt said quietly. "You are offering me extinction." He started for the door.

"You will regret your decision, Mr. Hewlitt." The voice followed after him. "This will be your only chance."

Hewlitt kept walking. It had been a long time since he had felt important, and he walked with dignity. As he closed the door, he could still hear the voice echoing, "This will be your only chance."

He walked through the large room where the men were working at their desks. No one glanced up. He felt sorry for them, especially for Ben. Ben had said no sacrifice was too great for his boys.

The elevator was waiting.

As Walter started to leave the building, he remembered that his rubbers were still upstairs. He crossed the lobby and retraced his steps down the quiet back corridor. But at the end of the hallway there was only a blank wall.

Walter rushed back down the hall and, squinting his eyes, peered up at the registry. There was no listing for the Atlas Company. He shook his head in disbelief as, slowly, understanding filtered into his mind. Perhaps some other man, sometime in the future, might be summoned to ride the elevator up. For him, however, the elevator to the fifty-fourth floor would never be there again.

Four in the Blast

A Veri-tale by Judith Davey

The wail of the air raid siren had barely died away when the first wave of German bombers appeared over London. Seconds later the bright summer day erupted with the whine of falling bombs, the explosions as they hit their targets, the crashing of buildings, and the crackle of anti-aircraft guns.

Ten-year-old Bertie, ambling along the street, whistling "Lili Marlene," glanced up at the blue sky. "Gor blimey! You blokes are in a 'urry today!" Hands in his pockets he scuffed along, kicking an imaginary football ahead of him. Only when the screaming of bombs had driven most people off the streets did he begin to look for a shelter. Quickening his pace only slightly, he turned the corner and saw the familiar "S."

I'll just pop in there a second, he thought. *Don't want to be late for me tea.*

Winding his way round the sandbags that covered the entrance, Bertie descended the stone steps into the basement of an old warehouse that had been converted into a public shelter. As his eyes adjusted to the gloom, he made out a large, windowless room with bare, crumbling cement walls, and benches along three sides. A lone twenty-five-watt bulb hung suspended on a chain from the ceiling. There were two other occupants in the shelter: a young girl in a brown dress, that matched her limp brown hair, and an elderly woman, leaning against the wall, her eyes closed.

"Afternoon, miss. Afternoon, grandma," Bertie said, remembering his manners.

"Mrs. Willis to you, my lad," the woman snapped. *Kids are all the same these days. No respect for their elders.*

She sighed, lost in her thoughts. *No gratitude either. What thanks did she get from her grandchildren when she went without her chocolate ration to save it for them? All they did was fight over it! Or her own children for that matter. Did it ever occur to Meg that her mum might be too tired to take care of the kids after working all day in the factory? Always gallivanting off some place, Meg was. Fire watching or some other duty. Ought to stay home with . . .*

The door of the shelter flew open, and a young man in air force uniform was almost blown into the room by the blast of a bomb.

"Phew!" Bertie exclaimed. "That was close! 'ow 'bout shutting the door, guv'ner? Think you can make it with your knees knockin' an' all?"

Mildred smoothed her brown hair and glanced at the boy. There was something appealing about his tight little face, his sassiness. She looked at the young officer, fatigue and strain clearly written in his face. *He looks scared,* she thought, *really scared.*

Pilot officer Tony Mills shakily closed the door and sat down as far from the boy as possible. *Damn Cockney brat! No manners. Just like all of them!*

He glanced briefly at the two women, then returned to his own pressing problem. *If only I could stop shaking! Nothing is going to happen! Not to me! Everyone in the squadron says so. Lucky Tony they call me. I wish I was up there in my Spitfire! I never shake up there—never! What was it that fellow said after Tom was shot down? "Jerry's going to get all of us sooner or later"? Well, the others, maybe. But not me. Not me.*

79

"Hear them bombs?" Bertie yelped gleefully. "Good an' safe down 'ere, eh guv?"

"Now stop that!" Mildred could no longer keep silent. *You can think whatever you like, but there is such a thing as respect.*

"About time your mum gave you a good hiding," Mrs. Willis added.

Bertie jumped up. "Nobody beats me, never!"

"Well, perhaps somebody should . . ."

Mrs. Willis' words were swallowed up in a tremendous explosion, that shook the old building to its foundation. Mildred and Bertie, lighter than the others, were knocked off the bench. Bits of plaster and fine grey dust floated down from the ceiling. The light bulb swung like a pendulum, but it didn't go out.

Bertie was the first to recover.

"Direct 'it!" he said, dusting himself off. *I'll catch it for getting me school clothes dirty,* he thought.

Mildred picked herself up, hurried across the room, and flung the door open, almost disappearing in a cloud of dust. When the dust had cleared, there was only blackness.

She gasped. The other three, joining her, stared into the blackness.

"It can't be!" Mrs. Willis cried. "It can't be dark. We haven't been here that long!"

Before anyone could stop him, Bertie jumped through the open doorway . . . and bounced right back, rubbing his nose.

"Cement! We're buried alive, that's what we are!"

Mildred gingerly closed the door, shutting out the darkness.

Mrs. Willis sat down quickly. *So it had finally happened. What she had been afraid of ever since the war started, more afraid of than dying–to be trapped, buried alive. Admittedly, she wasn't hurt or alone.* She breathed deeply, trying to control her terror, the pounding of her heart. *Keep calm,* she told herself. *Surely, we'll soon be found.*

Tony's first reaction was to get as far away from the others as possible. Alone, he huddled on a bench at the other end of the large room. Shaking, fighting the rising panic, he put his trembling hands between his quaking knees. He knew what they were all thinking. But he didn't care. He didn't care about anything any more.

Mildred glanced at the pathetic figure, hunched on the bench. *He's so frightened, poor young chap.*

I'm not afraid. Why not? And the boy? He doesn't seem to be frightened either.

Bertie, recovered from his painful encounter with the cement wall, was busily exploring the confines of the basement room that had become their prison.

Tony struggled to rouse himself. *I can't give in like this. I'm an RAF officer, I have an image to live up to. They'll expect me to take charge. But what can I do?* He looked around helplessly, unable to focus his thoughts. Then he noticed three steps on the other side of the room, leading up to a wooden door.

"That must be another door into the warehouse. Let's try it."

"Already did," Bertie announced. "Won't budge."

Damn the kid! Tony climbed the stairs and put all his weight against the door. The other three hurried to help, but to no avail. Silently, they returned to their seats. Again the building shuddered. A new shower of plaster and dust covered the room.

This is it, Mildred thought. *In a few minutes the ceiling will cave in. I hope it'll be quick. I hope it won't hurt. Mother will have to get her own supper tonight.* A small smile crossed her lips. *That'll be a change! And*

I'll stand up Harold! The first time he's asked me for a date. Why hasn't he asked me before? Perhaps he's just shy. She sighed. *He's as plain as I am. Well, I can't be choosy. Like mother says, without looks or personality it's best I just stay home with her.*

Another blast shook the building. All four dived under the benches, afraid to breathe, eyes on the ceiling. The bulb on its chain swung wildly, but it held. The four prisoners watched it sway to stillness. Dust drifted down from a sudden crack in the ceiling.

Then, unexpectedly, the All-Clear sounded. Mrs. Willis heaved a sigh of relief. Tony stared straight ahead. Mildred and Bertie grinned at each other.

"Nobody knows we're 'ere," Bertie observed wryly.

"You're the nastiest little brat I ever met!" Tony snapped.

"We're all going to die a 'orrible death of suff . . . suff . . . We'll choke!"

"Shut up!" Tony hissed.

"Don't take any notice of him." Mildred spoke with a calmness that belied her age. "He doesn't mean it."

"I do too mean it," Bertie protested. "We're all . . ."

"Think of your mum," interrupted Mrs. Willis. "She'd be very sad if you died."

Bertie frowned at Mrs. Willis. *She don't understand,* he thought. *Mum'd be glad if I died. She always says there's too many of us.*

"Me mum don't care," he said curtly, his eyes on the floor.

"All mothers care about their children," Mrs. Willis assured him."

"Not when there's seven!"

Mrs. Willis thought for a moment, "You're in the middle?"

"Bertie looked surprised. "How'd you know?"

She smiled softly. "I bet your mum is waiting with your tea right now!"

"I bet she give it to baby Alphie!" he answered, snatching back his belligerence.

Mildred studied his hard little face. *So that's what's eating at him! He thinks his mother doesn't love him. Perhaps she doesn't. He's in the middle, he's not important. The older ones may be working, adding to the income, the younger ones need more attention. That's why he isn't afraid.*

Suddenly, in that hard little face Mildred caught a glimpse of her own feelings. *Why . . . why I feel the same way! Mother doesn't care about me. The only one she cares about is Janet . . . beautiful Janet. I'm only her servant.* She straightened her shoulders and lifted her head. *If I come out of this alive I'll leave her. That's what I'll do. Live my own life. Maybe I'll join the ATS, drive a general around. Auxiliary Transport Service! That sounds grand! And I've always fancied the uniforms!*

She jumped up. "Let's try the door again. Perhaps we can dig ourselves out."

Tony, rousing himself with an effort, glanced at her in surprise. Her voice was firm and she no longer looked intimidated. He followed her to the entrance and tried the door. It had opened easily before, now it took their combined strength to pull it open, setting off an ominous rumbling. They stood back, hearts thumping, waiting for things to settle. Then, joined by Bertie and Mrs. Willis, they began to remove bricks and stones, careful not to set off any more rumbling. But for every chunk of cement they moved, two more tumbled down, filling the space. Sweating in the coolness of the basement, their hands scraped and bloody, they doggedly worked on, clearing the way inch by inch, till the cement wall stopped them.

Tony stepped back and dropped his hands to his sides.

"It's no use. We can't move that. Either someone finds us or we die here." He slammed the door, setting off the rumbling anew.

"Careful!" Mrs. Willis cried, all her fears returning. *I don't want to die yet! I want to see my grandchildren grow up. Little Betsy . . . such a pretty baby! And young Tommy–cheeky as he is, he's a smart chap.* Again, her heart started hammering. *I hope they're all right! I'll go there as soon as I get out of here.*

"Nobody knows we're 'ere," Bertie said again.

Mildred put a hand on his shoulder and felt him squirm. "You don't know that for sure. Someone may have seen us go in."

"My daughter Meg is an air raid warden. She says they check every shelter after a raid," Mrs. Willis put in.

"The only thing is, will the ceiling hold till they find us?"

"It'll come down when they start digging us out," Bertie announced.

"You morbid little squirt!" Tony shouted. He grabbed the boy by the shoulders and began to shake him fiercely. "Shut up! Do you hear? Shut up!"

Bertie tore himself free. "Gor blimey, guv! You've got it bad! If you don't watch out, you'll end up in the loony bin."

Both Mrs. Willis and Mildred held their breaths, afraid Tony would go after the boy. He started forward; then, struggling to control his trembling, he stopped and staggered back to his seat. *I've got to get away–far away. I'll ask for leave, long leave, not just a weekend. I can't go up there again . . . I can't. I've got to think of some excuse . . . But what? Sir, I'm afraid? Sir, it's my turn next? Sir, there's only two of us left in the squadron . . .*

"'ear that?" Bertie shouted suddenly.

"Hear what?"

"Sh! Listen!"

They held their breaths, listening. There was a sound, like distant knocking on metal.

Bertie rushed over to the water pipes in the corner. He banged on the pipes with his pocket knife, then listened.

"They want to know your names," he said.

"How do you know?" Mildred asked.

"Morse code."

"Where did you learn morse code?"

"Me dad taught me. 'e was a wireless operator on a bomber 'fore 'e was shot down. Pilot jumped out, me dad had no parachute."

Mrs. Willis looked at him. *Poor lonely kid. Nobody seems to care about him.* An unbearable longing to see her children and grandchildren spread through her body.

"I'm glad you're here," Mildred said to Bertie. "We couldn't have communicated without you."

"Yes, thank you," Mrs. Willis added.

Bertie pulled himself up to his full four and a half feet. "Don't mention it."

He continued to tap, listen, and answer.

"They'll 'ave us out in an 'our," he relayed. "They're waiting for a crane to pull up that big block out there."

Mrs. Willis' lips moved silently. Not a religious woman, she suddenly felt overwhelmed with a profound sense of gratitude. She would see her children and grandchildren again.

Tomorrow I'll join the ATS, Mildred thought. *Then I'll tell mother.*

Tony sat slumped over and silent. *So what?* he thought. *I wish the ceiling would cave in. I wouldn't have to face any more planes or guns or dead friends . . . or myself.*

Bertie was too intent on his new-found importance to have any thoughts at all. A light sound from the pipe caught his attention. He pressed his ear close. Then he turned to the others, his face flooded with disbelief.

"Me mum's out there. She come looking for me. For me!"

"I told you she would worry about you," Mrs. Willis said kindly.

"Looking for me!" Bertie repeated, stunned.

Soon they could hear the big crane at work. The building trembled and the light bulb swung back and forth. Then the door opened and a shaft of daylight lit up the shelter.

Mrs. Willis went through first, straight into the arms of her daughter.

"Oh, mum, you had us so worried! One of the shelters had a direct hit!"

Bertie stepped into the sunlight, hesitated a moment, squinting into the brightness. Uncertainty and brashness fell from him as he ran to his mother. She gave him a gentle shove. "'ere you are! You look a fine sight! Get a move on. Your tea's getting cold."

Mildred, smiling after Bertie, almost ran into Harold, who stood there awkwardly, waiting for her.

"How did you find me?"

"When you didn't come home, your mother rang the office. I was still there. I went looking for you, followed your route home. The bombed shelter had me a bit worried, but I was sure you weren't in that one." He smiled shyly.

Mildred smiled back. "You know what? I'm going to join the ATS."

Was it disappointment or respect that passed over Harold's face? Whichever, he took her arm and they started down the street together.

No one saw Tony leave.

Becoming the Chief

A Veri-tale by Tom Traub

S*o you think you're ready to become the chief.* You're twenty-four years of age, you've traveled and you've studied, you're smart and you're strong. Let me tell you about how Johnson Paul came to be the chief. Maybe then you'll see the situation a bit more clearly.

Johnson Paul was a strange child, possibly because he had a first name for a last name and a last name for a first name. He hated being called Paul Johnson, much as you'd hate being called by the reverse of your name, the way I'd hate being called Hammersmith Rusty. It's true that I am Johnson Paul's uncle, but I was also real good friends with the old chief, Mother Hatchet, so I'll tell you the story true, maybe making up some of the facts for a better telling, but getting the important parts right on the money.

Johnson Paul was born on April 19, 1965, which means he had his fiftieth birthday last spring. He was born right here in Tiboreaux, Louisiana, at the St. Thomas hospital, a big healthy baby who started right off squalling loud and pushing toys and blankets out of his bassinet. Johnson Paul needed a lot of room right away, and he's been that way ever since. His daddy, my brother-in-law, worked with me for H&R Block, two of the first black accountants in the South, living on the same street in what was then called the Negro Quarter. We'd put on our headdresses and buckskin pants every Mardi Gras and dance and holler and whoop; then the next week we'd be back behind our desks, wearing suits and ties. That's the way things were when Johnson Paul was growing up. Modern, but with the past—like Mother Hatchet—all around him.

Johnson got interested in magic very young. I don't mean real magic, I mean sleight-of-hand, card tricks, making a scarf change colors, and like that.

One day, when Johnson was twelve years old, he carried his magic kit down the street to where Mother Hatchet sat rocking on the front porch of her notions store. She never spent much time inside the store.

People would just go in and take what they wanted—
tea, coffee, spices, candy, a spool of thread—then put
their money in the coffee jar and take what change was
due. Every now and again some teenager might try to
get around Mother Hatchet, having paid insufficient
funds, just dropping in enough coins to make an
audible racket. Then they'd walk past Mother Hatchet,
some with a big cheery "Good morning!" some quiet,
like they wouldn't be noticed. Mother Hatchet would
say, "You sure you dropped off the right change in
there?" They'd go back in and make restitutions.
Never saw anyone argue, and when it wasn't tax season
I spent a lot of time on that porch with Mother
Hatchet.

So on this hot September day Johnson put on his
little magic show for Mother Hatchet and myself, as we
rocked on the porch. The road hadn't been paved yet,
and he stood in the dirt in his blue jeans and sneakers,
wearing an old, beat-up top hat and one of his daddy's
sport coats with the sleeves rolled up to his wrists.
Mother Hatchet just loved his act, laughing and
applauding. She played the back-country nigger for
him. He'd make little metal balls disappear and she'd
say, "Where dat go? Where be de shiny liddle ball?"
Then Johnson would guess a card she had picked and

she'd yell, "Lawd hep us, the young 'un must be possessed by de debbil!" For his big finale, Johnson held up a black lacquered wooden box. He unfolded it, showing that the box was empty. Then he folded it back up, passed a hand over it, and unfolded it, to show that a white dove had appeared inside.

But his finale was marred, because the dove had died. The boy must have left it in his coat pocket too long on that sweltering day, and the poor thing just lay in the box with its eyes open, dead as a stuffed deer head. Johnson sniffled back tears, he was so disappointed that his big show had fallen down. Mother Hatchet cooed at him and told him to bring the dove to her. He climbed the stairs and handed her the dead bird. She stroked it with hands as wrinkled and dry as tea leaves in a tin. She chanted at the bird, something like, "Maybe it isn't really dead, maybe it's just a little dead, maybe it's just lost its senses, maybe it's about to wake up, maybe it's waking up right now."

The dove's eyes blinked and it jumped up to its feet, standing on Mother Hatchet's palm. It shook out its wings, and she handed the bird back to Johnson. His eyes wide as zeroes, he took the bird and walked back up the street to his parents' house.

But Mother Hatchet underestimated Johnson. Because he was young and baby-faced, she assumed he'd believe that the dove had just been sleeping, or knocked out. But he knew that dove had been stone dead and Mother Hatchet had returned its life to it.

From that day on Johnson Paul lost his interest in fake magic and gained a fascination with real magic. He read all the books in the library; then he copied the bibliographies from the backs of those books and took his lists into New Orleans. I remember the boy had just turned fourteen when he rode a Greyhound bus all by himself, four hours each way, into the city of New Orleans. Armed only with a city map and the money he had saved from two years of delivering papers, he found every occult bookstore listed in one of his library books, and he bought as many used paperbacks as his money would cover.

Those books kept him for a while, but not that long. All through high school he studied, and he lived the way the books recommended. He became a vegetarian, which isn't easy around here; at dinner-time you're surrounded by crawfish stewing in gumbo, spicy fried chicken, sausage sizzling in jambalaya. But he did it. And all through high school his sport was boxing, so that he could eliminate physical fear from his character. He never did become even a halfway decent fighter, but so much the better. With every fight he lost, and there were four years of them, with every punch he took and every drop of blood he shed he became a little less afraid of pain, of punishment, of physical threat.

And the boy studied magic. About halfway through his junior year of high school, when Johnson was sixteen, he first sent his spirit out of his body. He flew over the whole town. A couple of weeks later, he flew—his spirit, of course—into his math teacher's office, where he read the test that was slated for the following day.

He got the ability to move things, make a paper clip stand up and walk, end over end, across a desk. His dreams became prophetic. And sometimes he'd visit me in my dreams, wanting to know about the family history, things more true than can be spoken about in waking words.

He noticed a fact that most young people failed to notice: that whoever was our representative in the Louisiana legislature, whoever was our alderman in the city council, whoever was the richest black person in our part of town, the person who actually ran the Negro Quarter was Mother Hatchet. By that time we were called the Black section, the way ten years later we would become the African-American neighborhood; but whatever we were called, the person in charge, year after year, was Mother Hatchet.

Say there was a vote about having a street light installed. The alderman might come around, visit the barbershop and Leon's Bar, the restaurants and beauty parlors; he might ask how we felt about spending two thousand dollars on a traffic light for the intersection of Cecil Avenue and Bourque Street. Somewhere along his tour he'd stop in front of Mother Hatchet's rocker, take out a handkerchief and wipe the sweat off the back of his neck, and say something like, "Why, Mother Hatchet. Have you heard tell about this controversy? What's your opinion about it?" He'd be very casual, amused, even condescending to Mother Hatchet, but whatever she said, that is what would happen—"Yes" or "No" or "I don't give a damn." When St. Mary's hired a new priest, he was cleared by Mother Hatchet; when some young stud became a problem, it was Mother Hatchet who arranged for his luck to run out.

The day that Johnson graduated high school he presented himself, still in his nice blue suit and shiny shoes, at Mother Hatchet's porch. I'd been at the ceremony and now I was sitting there on her porch, drinking some cool lemonade, passing the time of day with Mother Hatchet, when Johnson offered himself as her assistant.

She said, "I don't need no assistant."

That flustered Johnson. I guess the way a boy whose daddy's a farmer expects that he'll be a farmer, in the back of his mind Johnson always assumed he'd work for Mother Hatchet.

Johnson tried to make the best of it, salvage something of his dream. He said, "When you do need an assistant, will it be me?"

Mother Hatchet laughed. They must have been twelve feet apart, her on the porch and him on the street, but she seemed to laugh right in his face. She said, "I'll need an assistant when they pull my dead body off this porch. I'll need an undertaker's assistant!" Then she laughed again.

I felt torn between wanting to help my sister's boy, who I was very fond of, and standing by Mother Hatchet, who was the brains and heart of our community. I just sat there, watching it all and memorizing every detail.

I saw Johnson's face getting flushed. Even the darkest black people visibly blush, but our family has so much white in it—you just need to look at my hair, which is why I'm called Rusty—that we actually get sort of pinkish-brown when we're upset or angry, and Johnson looked plenty of both.

Real slowly, choking back his emotions, Johnson said, "That undertaker might be here a lot sooner than you think, if you don't stop driving yourself so hard and take on an assistant. I can feel your power, Mother Hatchet, and I'm not challenging you. I'm just saying, why don't you let me take over the little stuff for you, the drudgery . . ."

He had threatened with the stick, now he was going to tempt with the carrot, but Mother Hatchet wouldn't let him hold either a stick or a carrot out to her and get away with it. She looked at the young man, her eyes bugging out, a look that would have driven a dog insane or made a frog explode. Johnson met her look but didn't really engage her. His eyes were shut off from his soul; he had put up a block against any power going in or any power going out.

Mother Hatchet relaxed back into her chair and nodded, like she'd won already. She said to me, from the corner of her mouth, "Rusty, this young stud thinks he's a full-grown man. Take him into the store and give him a lollipop."

I nodded and pushed to my feet. Johnson looked up at me, trying to wound me with his hurt eyes, his sense of betrayal. By my obeying Mother Hatchet, Johnson thought I had betrayed him and our family. I lifted my hands up, slow and easy, a sign for him to relax, cool down.

He came up the steps without deigning to look at Mother Hatchet. Then he stepped into the cool, dark store with me. I knew what he wanted was conversation, not a lollipop, but I took him to the candy counter. I reached down behind the counter and brought up a dusty jar and forced a place for it between the licorice sticks and the jaw breakers. Inside this big glass jar was just one dead, dried-out grasshopper.

Johnson pointed one of his skinny fingers at the insect—he was so surprised he forgot his anger—and he asked, "What's this?"

I put my hand on the top of the jar and said, "This was your uncle Byford, who tried to kill Mother Hatchet with a shotgun about twenty years ago, when he was just about your age."

If Johnson had blushed red before, he blanched white now—he could have played eighteen holes at any country club in New England. The color took a long time returning to his face. He unscrewed the lid of a different jar and took out a bright cherry lollipop. With trembling hands he pulled off the wrapper as I put away the remains of my brother Byford. Johnson stuck the lollipop in his mouth and all but ran out of the store—I remembered to drop a dime into the coffee can for him. For ten years my last sight of Johnson was his dark silhouette hurrying out into the afternoon sun from the notions store.

He sent letters and snapshots home to his mother, saying he was fine and telling how he was getting along. For a while he made a living reading Tarot cards at Renaissance Faires. With his hair grown out into dreadlocks he brought in a couple of boats from Jamaica, precognating where the Coast Guard wouldn't be. He did this and did that, a young man learning the world, and all along he practiced magic. He studied in Jamaica, he studied in Haiti, he studied gritty street magic in Harlem, and he finished his training only a hundred miles away, studying wet, green magic in the Atchafalaya Swamp.

In the year 1993, at twenty-eight years of age, Johnson Paul returned to Tiboreaux. He had changed in every visible way, yet deep down inside he remained the same. An inch or two taller, many pounds heavier, he wore blue jeans and hiking boots and one of those rough, white sweatshirts from Mexico. He had Rasta dreadlocks past his shoulders, a beard and a mustache, a silver skull dangling from one ear, and a silk scarf rolled into a cord and wrapped around his head. It was hard to know what he looked like—something like a pirate, but also like a pothead guitar player. He looked successful but shady, dangerous but trustworthy. He looked like what he was, a man who had returned to his hometown for a showdown.

Johnson's mother threw him a big dinner the first night he was home. He was still eating vegetarian, but the rest of us weren't so particular. We ate up fried prawns stuffed with crab, roast turkey and gravy, red beans cooked with garlic and onions, sweet potato and marshmallow pie, and we drank cold bottles of Crescent City beer with wedges of lime stuffed in the bottle necks. There was lots of laughter and slaps on the back, lots of kidding about his Bob Marley hair, lots of *ooh's* and *ah's* for the presents he brought back. Johnson gave his momma a broach shaped like a blackbird with a ruby eye, and he gave his daddy an emerald tie clip. His daddy wore that tie clip to work every day until he died, and then he wore it to his grave. All the relatives filled Johnson in on what had been happening, and we heard many stories from him about what he'd been doing: a lot of women, a lot of traveling, a lot of play, and a lot of work.

During a lull after dinner he asked to speak to me alone, so we went out to the garage and sat on stools at his daddy's work bench. It was a cold night—I wore a sweater under my sport coat—but he seemed comfortable in his Mexican sweatshirt.

He picked up a handful of ten-penny nails. In the palm of his hand they softened like warm crayons. They merged into each other, then melted into a puddle like dark quicksilver. He poured the metal onto the workbench, where it congealed into a flat blob of iron. He picked it up and dropped it into the metal trash basket, where it landed with a clang.

Looking into my eyes, he said, "I've returned for my confrontation with Mother Hatchet."

I nodded. It hadn't taken Sherlock Holmes to deduce that one.

"I'm not asking you if I'm ready, if I'm powerful enough, because I know that I am. I'm asking you if you will stand by me, stand with the family, or if you will be on her side."

I spread my hands, helplessly neutral, feeling very soft and vulnerable, sitting next to this man who had so hardened his mind and body. I said, "I want the best for you, and for the family, and for the community. I don't know if what's best for any of us is that you kill Mother Hatchet. I sure don't want her killing you. Maybe you could find some other town where you'd be more needed."

Johnson shook his head, the dreadlocks wiggling like snakes. "Here is my town and my people; here is my source. So you won't fight for me, or against me?"

I nodded again, and he nodded, too.

"That's all I ask." He tapped a fingertip against the counter, then he looked back at me. "Uncle, I have the power. Uncle Byford must have thought he had the power. Do you have the power?"

I shook my head, smiling down at the sawdust on the cracked concrete floor. "I've never had even a hint of the power. I'm like a person who loves music but can't play an instrument or sing a note. I've been around magic all my life, and I might someday make a contribution to the study, but it sure won't be as a magician." We headed back inside for more beer and stories.

The next day was cool and cloudy, rain starting and stopping. I was sitting on the porch with Mother Hatchet, my hands wrapped round a mug of tea, when Johnson appeared in the street, looking just as he had last night. Mother Hatchet finished the sip of tea she was taking, before putting down her mug and looking at him.

She said, "You're not ready to fight me, Johnson."

He said, "If you don't defend yourself, then you will surely die."

The screen door swung open behind me. I looked over my shoulder and watched as a child walked out of the store, a child who was Johnson Paul at twelve years of age, wearing his daddy's sport coat with the sleeves rolled up and a battered top hat. Mother Hatchet parted her knees. The boy stood in front of her, looking out at the adult Johnson Paul, as Mother Hatchet put a hand on the boy and drew him to her, pressing his back against her chest.

"Attack away, sonny boy," she said. Then she laughed that unpleasant laugh.

Johnson seemed totally bewildered, like he didn't know what to do, or even what to think. Was this really him, in the flesh, as a child? If he directed an attack at Mother Hatchet, could she redirect it at his earlier self? If his earlier self was killed, would he disappear?

Johnson turned around and walked out of town. He'd had the power for a killing blow, he'd had the power to force through Mother Hatchet's defense, but not the knowledge necessary to understand the implications. So he went off again, again for ten years. Last time he had accumulated strength. This time it was wisdom he was after. Johnson cut off his dreadlocks, put on a suit and tie, and got jobs teaching at universities. He taught French at Louisiana State University, he taught African-American History at the University of California at Berkeley, he taught acupuncture at Johns Hopkins, and he taught a course in Louisiana politics at Dartmouth.

Everywhere he went he learned as well as taught. He learned by teaching and taught by learning. He studied magic, of course, but he also studied history and politics, philosophy and theology. He learned physics. He learned about time, and space, and matter, and energy.

During those ten years he got married and had a son and a daughter, learning about love and affection and responsibility.

He returned in the summer of two thousand and three. I had retired the year before from H&R Block and now spent all my days on the porch with Mother Hatchet. Johnson now had a bit of a pot belly and a bald spot. He wore a three-piece suit with a gold watch chain hanging from the vest pocket. Again, he looked totally different and yet, deep down, the same. Again he spent a day and a night with the family, introducing his children to their many uncles and aunts and cousins, and again he appeared at Mother Hatchet's porch the next afternoon.

That day was so hot and muggy it was like living in a bubbling fish stew. I'd brought Mother Hatchet an ice cream cone, and we were sitting in rockers, racing our ice creams as they melted, trying to lick up the dribbles before they fell to the floor.

"Good day, Mother Hatchet."

"Hello, sonny boy."

Johnson folded his fleshy hands in front of himself, gazing up at her coolly. "If you produce an earlier avatar of myself, Mother Hatchet, I'll kill it, along with you, knowing that if, by killing it, I died as a boy, then I won't be here to kill myself, and I will live. Reach deep into your bag of tricks, old witch, because one of us doesn't see the sunset tonight."

She threw her half-eaten cone over the side railing, then clutched her gnarled hands on the arms of her rocker, staring at Johnson. With an odd, indignant creak, the rocker rose up off the floorboards and hovered about two feet off the porch. Slowly, like a strip of fly paper turning in a light wind, the rocker rotated around so that Mother Hatchet faced the front of the store. The rocker settled back down slowly, then completely, as the spell collapsed.

"Go ahead, sonny boy," she yelled. "Attack away."

Johnson's eyes flicked to me, then to the old woman's back.

"Go ahead. Kill me. Kill me while my back's turned. You know what'll happen then? You think you'll be respected? You'll be thought of as a viper, a snake that struck from behind 'cause he couldn't win a fair fight. You think people will come to you? People will still talk about me. They'll say, 'What would Mother Hatchet have thought about this?' You'll just mark time, sonny, till a real chief comes along."

She looked over her bony shoulder, her face peeking out from the back of the rocker.

"But I'll tell you what I'll do. You want a fight, you been itchin' for one since you were in school, I'll give you one. In ten years. Come back here in ten years and I'll give you your fight, and I'll kick your tail. That's the deal."

In Johnson's face I saw the indecision, the temptation to strike right then and settle things, one way or the other. I also saw the knowledge that a challenger fights on the champion's terms, where she wants, when she wants. He looked at me, and I nodded, playing my part in the history of magic as a referee.

With his wife and children Johnson settled in Tiboreaux, learning something more valuable than strength or wisdom, learning patience. In the next ten years he became a full professor at the University of Southwestern Louisiana. He wrote a book about the peoples in this area that's still used as a text book at the university. His son started at his old high school. He began work on another book.

One hot afternoon three years ago, Johnson was walking down the street on his way to visit his widowed mother. He tipped his hat as he walked past Mother Hatchet's porch, where she and I were sipping some cool apple juice, talking about the old days.

She called out, "Hey, sonny boy! It's been ten years, today."

Johnson stopped like he'd walked into a glass wall. He turned and faced us and thought for a moment.

"That's okay, Mother Hatchet. I don't really want your place any more. You're doing fine, a good job. I've got my own affairs now."

He started to turn away.

"Chicken?" she taunted.

He looked back, smiling. "No. Uninterested."

Again, he turned away.

The old woman got up from her rocker. "In that case," she said, "the job is yours."

And with that she walked into the store, climbed the stairs to her bedroom, lay down on her bed, and died.

She left everything to Johnson Paul. There was some delay while the state's attorney searched for a Paul Johnson, but after repeated explanations Johnson Paul got everything: the store, the porch, the rocker. He got several chests of mysterious objects—mysterious to most people. He got shelves full of books. And he got a glass jar, containing a desiccated grasshopper.

Johnson had me tend the store till at fifty he retired from teaching. Then he took full-time to the rocker and the town's business, as the hand-picked successor to Mother Hatchet.

And now you, child, you tell me you want to challenge Johnson Paul. What I say to you is this: Don't do it. If he likes you, the best you'll get is a thirty-year unpaid apprenticeship. If he doesn't like you, the way Mother Hatchet didn't like my brother Byford, you could wind up about as long as my finger, with wings and six legs, living out the rest of your life at the bottom of an empty candy jar.

Family Tree

A Veri-tale by Robert U. Montgomery

Michael hadn't known what he was going to say until he said it. He had known only that he was depressed and he needed to walk. But here in the cathedral of the woods, on a rock very much like a pulpit, he spoke.

"I loved a tree, but not my father."

As if he could not believe what he had heard, he said it again.

"I loved a tree, but not my father."

Suddenly, he was shouting.

"I loved a tree, but not my father!"

Then he sat down on the rock, overlooking a stream, and he cried.

How could a person love a tree, but not his father?

"I love you." A year ago Michael had said the words, as he held the cold hand of a man who in a few minutes would die. He had never before said them to his father, just as his father had never said them to him.

He felt guilty saying the words, for he didn't feel them, even then. But he remembered reading that people often experience regret when they neglect to make peace with the dying. And he decided guilt would be better than regret. Besides, his mother and his sister expected him to say the words. Doing so would help keep the peace.

Michael plunged his hands into his coat pockets and thought about why he didn't love his father, a depressed alcoholic with a violent temper.

Mom always told me that he loved me. But never once did he tell me himself. Mom said he bragged about me to the people he worked with. But never once did he tell me, "I'm proud of you."

Michael remembered the day he caught his first big bass. He ran into the house, yelling, "Dad, Dad! Come see what I caught!"

His father got up from the chair that he lived in when he wasn't at work. He walked to the back door, took one look at the fish, and said, "Is that all you caught?"

He remembered the times, when he was very little, that his father had spanked him, hard, with a belt, and how once, when he was eight, the spanking had turned into a beating. Across the breakfast table his father had teased him: "I hear that Susie kissed you. Did you like it?" Michael had gotten upset, accidentally spilling a glass of milk, and his father had exploded. "You'll pay for that!" he had yelled, as he took off his belt. He thrashed his back, his bottom, his legs, raising angry red welts across his whole skinny body.

After that, whenever we were in a room together, I was always more comfortable with someone or something between us.

But yes, his father had been a good provider. He worked long, hard hours at a job he never liked. They had never wanted for anything.

My father gave me food, shelter . . . and fear. He never gave me love.

Michael looked down at his reflection. It seemed to be staring back, as if it had a life of its own and had been caught off guard, like a mirror image, captured in a quick glance.

The tree had been a part of Michael's life for twenty-five years. It was a small tree, just about his size, when they moved to the house where his mother lived now, alone.

Michael decorated the pine that first Christmas, and every year thereafter, until it grew too tall for him to reach the upper branches.

As the tree continued to grow, it provided nest sites for more and more birds each spring. Its shade kept the yard cool in summer, and the leaves grew so thick he could stand under them in a summer squall and never get wet. In the fall it dropped its pinecones, just in time for making Christmas decorations. And in winter, with snow piled upon its boughs, it stood as a stark tribute to the harsh beauty of nature.

Aside from his family, the tree was the longest constant in Michael's life, and unlike his father, it provided only happy memories.

It was always there for me. It never hurt me.

Then, one fall day, two weeks ago, he had driven up to his mother's house, to find the tree had been cut down. "The needles and pinecones made too much of a mess," she said. And that was the end of it.

Michael grieved that night, and for several days after—grieved as he had not grieved for his father. And that was what had sent him searching.

Looking down at his image, reflected in the stream, Michael struggled to understand why he could love the tree and not his father.

No one should feel that way.

He shook his head slowly.

No one should love an object more than a person.

But rationalizing wasn't the answer. It only hid the truth and delayed its discovery.

He stared down into the clear, cold pool. Just then, a wind stirred the water, and as it flattened again, he saw within it the reflection of a tree. "That's not my pine," he said. But still he felt the warmth associated with his tree.

The wind stirred the water again. This time Michael's attention was drawn back to his own reflection. "There's no doubt about it. Physically, I am my father's son." But the realization did not reassure him, and it helped not at all with his dilemma.

He looked again. The reflection seemed to have grown older. He could see gray hair and wrinkles. Or was it just the wind-blown water, distorting his reflection? A chill ran down his back.

"Dad? Is that you?"

He closed his eyes, sucked in his breath, and began to talk to his father as he never had done before.

"Yes, Dad, I loved it. I loved the tree. It was tall and straight. It did everything a tree was supposed to do. And it never frightened me either. It was easy to love. It was lovable."

He paused, clenching his eyes against the wind, his fists against his anger, and his heart against his longing.

"After your first heart attack you cared so little about yourself that you went right on drinking and smoking." He was talking faster now. "You didn't like yourself, and that kept you from showing love for anyone else . . . for me. The tree wasn't like that, Dad. . . ." Suddenly, he stopped, his words echoing back on the wind. "The tree wasn't like that. . . ."

Of course, it wasn't. Trees don't love us—at least not in the way we understand. They're just trees. We love them just for being what they are.

And suddenly, in the echoes of the wind, Michael found his answer.

You don't have to get love to be able to give love. The tree never loved me, but I loved the tree.

Michael opened his eyes. "Dad? Dad?" But his Dad was gone. The reflection was his again. Or maybe it was a reflection of both of them—the best part, of both of them—the part that had not died.

Harvest

A Veri-tale by David E. Shapiro

Oh, they plowed him in a furrow deep,
Till the clods lay upon his head,
And these three then made a solemn vow,
That John Barleycorn was dead.

They left him there for a week or two,
Till a shower of rain did fall.
Then John Barleycorn sprang back up again,
And so proved them liars all.

— traditional song

A black-hooded, black-cloaked figure is drifting along
a residential street. Even its skeletal fingers are hidden
in darkness. They grip the long, ebony handle which
supports the one menacingly bright point on the

apparition: a sharp, glinting scythe blade. The figure evanesces, and invisibly takes up station inside a modest home in the middle of the block.

John and Barbara are in bed, loving, but also striving. It isn't quite the fun it used to be, when they were two. Now they are both two and one. Older, they still make glad love. But they desperately want to have a child, and they're afraid they can't.

Barbara's fingers are partly curled, her palm against John's chest. She runs the backs of her nails up through the pale, curly hairs extending from his lower ribs to just below his collarbone. As she does, she frets just a little. When they were younger, she recalls, the killjoy was her worry about what they would do if their contraception failed. Now it's the reverse. Being more serious people, their hopes and fears are also more serious. She pulls tight against his body with her other arm, trapping her hand against his chest. Over her heart, over his.

John is enjoying the feel of his hip against Barbara's warm thigh, the chill of her nails teasing his chest, and the beginning of a responsive tension in his groin. His mind touches on the hoped-for product of their love-making as well as on the delicious now of process. John is hoping they'll have a boy, someone he can watch having all the fun he remembers—and some of the fun he missed out on, too. A son will be someone he can guide, someone he can teach all the things that he learned as a kid. But maybe a boy would rebel against him. The Oedipal thing, siding with his mother. A girl would be nice, too. He pulls Barbara's head softly to nestle against his chest, and she nuzzles him.

Barbara settles her leg around him more securely, as she thinks along parallel lines. And she thinks about names, and about her friends' children, and about her relationship with her mother.

With a clench of concern in her belly, she wonders how hard it will be for her to carry a child at her age.

The black-shrouded figure has looked in on this scene of nascent creation from the very first. From before the very first.

The primordial confusion swirls, undifferentiated. But the figure is there. Swuush! The scythe cuts free a galaxy, killing the early oneness and creating identity. Color and shape provide definition.

It is the first galaxy, as much an orphan as a galaxy could be. First harvest is ever the sacrifice.

A sun grows fat and hot and pregnant, distended with strange new elements. The time has come for this part of its life-cycle to end, for the new to come forth out of its substance. The figure shifts, the ebony handle swings, and Swuush! The scythe releases a supernova, and brings forth sulfur and nitrogen and iron and carbon, which some day will form a planet.

Life is more poignant. The dark figure is eternally witnessing, eternally alone. It identifies with striving, with intelligence. With every "I am." For that defines its kin.

The first amoeba forms and—Swuush!—dies. Becomes again indistinguishable from its ground substance. But it changes that substance in its ending as it had in its living. Then another amoeba forms, and flourishes. Taking in what it needs from the slowly moving waters, it swells.

The figure bears witness as, distended, the amoeba starts to bulge. The scythe cuts—Swuush!—and the bulge is gone from its side. The reaper's slicing follow-through is at the same time a reverent bow. Now another amoeba, newly-formed, floats alongside the first. Never again is it one, but always now separate, defined as separate by the boundaries that absolutely limit its connection to its fellow. Is Two better than One, because Two allows sharing and contact? Is Two worse than One, because Two allows alienation?

In that modest home in the middle of the block the reaper again serves duty. Barbara's ovaries say goodbye to little bits of herself, eggs that are her offerings to the universe outside her flesh: to the Other. John's testes do similarly, serving in his own fight against the knowledge of dark isolation, proclaiming that same wired-in faith in sending forth Something.

A spermatozoon isolates itself from the swimming swarm of its fellows. Frenetically wiggling far from its companions, it risks aloneness. And its brave *I am* succeeds, as it finds unity with the descended egg. Swuush! Each ends its identity then, in their merger. The dark, fearsome presence in the room honors equally the galactic and the microscopic. Rearing high, it cuts mercilessly, fulfilling the promise inherent in all existence.

The fertilized egg is a new creation, whose brief existence may soon be snuffed entirely. Like the unsuccessful swimmers, the unkissed eggs, it may tumble to nothingness like the earlier amoeba. Or else its separate identity may once again be cut short like those of its progenitors. It may cease its free-floating existence, modeled on that of the amoeba. It may exchange that life to mimic the proto-planet, whose very chemistry is ceded by the sun whose substance it suckles.

The watching figure is anonymous; the process, inexorable. But yet . . . as so many times before, the reaper muses. Can John and Barbara accept the growth of another being, another non-self? Or does each really expect to reproduce, to find self outside self? Looking into them, the reaper sees hope. Sees cause for hope.

John lies calmly after coitus, but his mind is not fully still. He has some regrets, thinking of the times when he was younger and could easily have fathered crowds—if spreading his seed were fathering. He gently strokes Barbara's side, long strokes, from her head down to her legs. He tempers his regret, recognizing that he was a different person when he was younger. That John is the person out of whom his present self grew, and one with whom he feels much connection; but not the same John. Not the man now cherishing Barbara. And hoping.

Barbara feels warm inside, and very soft. Very loved. She, too, is hoping that something will happen this time, but she shares his balance, his perspective. Come what may, she will never be too agonizingly alone, because her husband acknowledges her *I am*.

The reaper looks deeper. This couple has continued for all their years together to build a relationship by discovery, by consensus, rather than each hanging blindly and cruelly onto old assumptions. Neither has ignored the Otherness of the other.

Still, the watching figure does not pre-judge, even if the experiences of eons have fostered a strong interest. A twist, a firm, chopping—Swuush! The scythe brings forth an extra dose of progesterone. The so recently-created fertile egg implants itself in the warm, rich wall of the womb. Its short-lived separate identity terminated by the action of the deadly scythe, it is now one with Barbara.

Several months pass. The egg splits and splits again. The mass of cells start to lose their appearance of identity, and specialized tissues appear. Nerve cells. A brain, and organized control signals. This being remains parasitically attached to Barbara until her uterus sends it forth into the universe in the equivalent of a supernova. But weeks before then there is a working cortex: another human begins to create itself. And eventually blesses the harvest: says, "*I.*"

Swuush!

A Quality Piece

A Veri-tale by Brenda RickmanVantrease

The yellow lights of the electric sign on Route 19N announced with blinking urgency to all passers-by that they were about to miss BOB AND BETTY'S AUCTION BARN AND RETAIL OUTLET — AUCTION EVERY FRIDAY NITE — 7 TIL ?

Beat-up Chevys and newer pick-ups lined the two-lane blacktop, some perched precariously, leaning into the ditch that marked the boundaries, others angling dangerously onto the shoulder, slowing down traffic as if by design.

Inside the concrete-block barn the crowd had already gathered, filling the battered folding chairs and even the two front-row couches which Bob had reluctantly condemned as "too dilapidated even to unload on the ole pack-rat Maud."

That inveterate community eccentric was at that very moment settling into her favorite spot near the snack corner, where coffee, candy, and cellophane-wrapped confections of dubious freshness were offered for sale. She positioned a cardboard box between brogan-clad feet and rummaged in the pocket of a skirt stamped with the merest memory of a flower print.

Nine-year-old Alice watched in disgust as the old woman munched with satisfaction on a GooGoo candy bar and paused to adjust her upper plate before throwing the wrapper on the floor. Other regulars, mostly farm laborers and mill workers in dirty jeans, shoes caked with red clay, lounged by the door, one flicking cigarette ash onto the concrete floor, another grinding out a butt under his heel.

"Grown-ups are real pigs," Alice thought. "If his kid threw something on the floor, he'd probably be hollerin' at her like a stuck hog."

She reached for the broom and the box-top that served as a dust pan and began to clumsily retrieve the offending refuse. Tossing a straw-colored braid behind her back, she leaned the broom against the wall and handed the yokel, who had already lit another cigarette, the little foil ash tray from the counter.

"Well, 'scuse me, Blondie." The man grinned an ugly grin, exposing long, stained teeth in an unshaven face. "Feisty little thing, ain't she?" he drawled.

Alice felt her face redden as she bent to pick up the candy wrapper. She wrinkled her sharp little nose. What was that peculiar musty odor that always followed old Maud? It was more than not taking enough baths or just the smell of sweat. That smell she recognized. Lots of times Bob would smell real sweaty after he had been chopping weeds in the "truck patch." That was his name for the ragged rows of corn and beans planted between the frame house and the concrete-block box he called the "auction barn."

When Bob would come in, all smelly, her mother would call him a pig and tell him to take a bath. She'd laugh in that kind of flirty way she had and say that she wasn't gonna be friendly with no man that stunk like a barnyard.

Bob always gave in to Betty when she talked in that whispery-whiny voice. When he came out of the shower, scrubbed red and smelling like Old Spice, Betty would start kissing on him. Sometimes they'd lock the bedroom door and Alice would hear strange noises—giggles, squeals, and grunts. They were friendly a lot, Alice thought.

But it wasn't sweat that she smelled now. Old Maud smelled different—like an unused room that had been shut up too long. That must be what it smelled like to be old—really old—not like Bob, who, although he had gray hair, was just middle-old, but old like the rocks and the red dirt in the clay hills behind their place. And moldy—like the grave. She wondered idly if God smelled like that. No. God, or at least Jesus, she reckoned, would have to smell sweet even though they were old. Wouldn't they? That was a good question for the Sunday School teacher at Mt. Olivet.

She would ask Miss Bishop the very next Sunday. That is, if Bob would let her go. Sometimes, when he was being ornery, he would fuss and threaten not to let her go, even though Miss Bishop always picked her up.

"That bunch of damn holy-rollers could mess up her mind," he would grumble.

Alice cringed at the memory. His talk was trashy. That was the truth. Lots of times he used words worse than "damn" or "hell." He talked just like white trash. Even as she thought it, Alice wondered what was the difference between white trash and colored trash. Trash was just trash, wasn't it?

"It's no skin off your backside if she goes to Sunday School," her mother would answer smartly, and then she would whisper something in his ear.

He would grin and say, "Well, I guess a little religion couldn't hurt ever now and again."

Betty had some kind of strange power over Bob that Alice couldn't quite understand. Nevertheless, she was glad to get to go. She liked going to Sunday School and she especially liked Miss Bishop. She always dressed real neat and her voice was soft and even. Alice couldn't imagine Miss Bishop screaming and cussing or talking in the whispery-whiny voice that Betty used. She liked the Bible stories too. It was nice to think about Jesus and Heaven, especially after Betty and Bob had one of their knock-down fights because Bob had come home drunk. She was sure that nobody ever got drunk in Heaven. Or smelled like a moldy grave, she reflected, as she glanced again at old Maud. She shuddered inwardly as her broom brushed Maud's box.

She shivered outwardly, too, from the cool blast cutting through the stale air as the door opened. She looked up to see a man and a woman that she hadn't seen before. Not regulars. What Bob called "fresh meat."

With her already practiced eye she tagged them as "city folk, out-of-towners," certainly not locals.

The man stopped at the counter to sign up. He pocketed the little square of paper with the bid number 87 scrawled in black marker and looked around for seats. The woman sniffed unappreciatively at the air heavy with smoke.

Alice was suddenly acutely aware of the clutter around her, of the broken furniture and the boxes, crammed with odds and ends, piled haphazardly around the periphery of the room. She noticed for the first time the ugliness of the jagged crack outlined with gray tape in the plate glass window. She stepped consciously in front of the hand-lettered sign, thumbtacked to the plywood podium, that baldly declared "All sales final — merchundize not picked up in 24 hrs. will be re sold."

"Antiquers. City slickers." Big Betty grinned.

Big Betty—that's what everybody called Alice's mother who, on the whole, accepted the sobriquet with robust good humor, especially when her husband accompanied the nickname with a playful pinch to her ample bottom or some other plump portion of her generous frame.

Big Betty gave Alice a sly wink as she summed up the newcomers. Alice hoped they didn't notice and pretended to ignore her mother's rudeness by directing her blue eyes downward in embarrassed contemplation of her scuffed loafers.

It wasn't that Alice didn't like her mother. They got on pretty good. She was the baby, and even a mite spoiled by some standards. "My little surprise package in my middle age," her mother often called her, as she'd tweak her daughter's pointed chin.

Even Bob petted her in his gruff way, though he wasn't her real father. She had never seen her real father, except, of course, in her imagination. In her imagination he was a god; tall, good-looking and sophisticated, like the men the women yearned after in her mother's soap operas. And, he was totally devoted to his beautiful daughter.

Bob called her his little "hustler" and paid her five dollars to help with the Friday night auctions. But she didn't do it for the money. She did it because she liked it. It was like playing store, only better, because she got to play with grown-ups, and that made it seem more real.

Her mother's laugh echoed across the room. Alice looked nervously at the out-of-towners. She wished her mother wouldn't laugh that way. And why did she talk so loud? And there was something about the way she put on her make-up, careless-like. Her lips were too red, and all that black eye-liner made her look like a raccoon. The way her face was marked by a brownish line where it joined her neck made Alice feel a little sick.

Alice stole a glance at the couple. She tried to analyze what it was that made them different from the rest of the crowd. For one thing, the man's shoes were not only clean but shiny, and she could tell that the jacket was buttery soft. It must be real leather, not imitation like Bob's. The woman murmured something to the man, who laughed softly.

"Alice!" Big Betty bellowed her name into the microphone. The way she said the "a" made its nine-year-old owner cringe. Her name sounded so pretty the way Miss Bishop said it.

"If my kid will come up to the front, we'll get started on this here sale." The microphone popped and sputtered as Betty slid it closer to her face.

Alice came forward to assume her position in front of the auctioneer's plywood platform, while her mother explained the house rules.

"We wanna welcome y'all to our regular Friday night auction. Y'all came to find a bargain and we've got lots of 'em. We're gonna start the bidding with this fine music box that Alice is holding."

Alice was almost in front of the couple. She noticed they were whispering again. Again, the man's soft laughter and a wink to his companion. Betty began the sale in the familiar cadence, while Bob worked the crowd.

"Yep," he'd call out with each bid, throwing up his arm and pointing to the bidder.

"Quarter, quarter, quarter. I got two-fifty for this fine music box. Two-seventy-five, anybody give two-seventy-five?"

She paused, and Bob interjected: "Yer goin' way wrong here. This here's a fine piece—all wood—plays 'Tennessee Waltz'."

He reached over and turned the key. The tinny notes drifted down, as Alice held the music box high over her head for the crowd to see.

Occasionally, she would acknowledge a front row bid with a timid, piping "Yep!" in imitation of her mentor. That she took her job seriously was affirmed by her rigid posture, the no-nonsense look in her blue eyes, and the thin line of her lips, pressed into an intense expression of earnestness.

The bidding had ended and the music box had finally brought seven dollars. Bob busied himself handing out a dozen music boxes to the crowd at the bidder's price. Alice knew that meant he was pleased with the bid, or he would not have let the others go.

"Number 37 gets a deal," he bellowed. "Number 42 gets a deal."

Betty was busy recording with her pad and pencil while Bob handed out the "deals." Alice watched his fat belly, flopping in the faded red shirt, so tight that it showed a little round indention where his belly button was buried and a white line of flesh where the shirt didn't quite cover the intended expanse. Bob's fat reminded her of cold, lumpy oatmeal. She could see the bulges, hanging over his belt, marked with a dirty line where the protrusion came into immediate contact with any surface he approached. If he lifted a box or a table, his belly inevitably got there before him. His dirty jeans bagged, secured precariously by the wide western belt with its confederate buckle.

He wiped sweat from his forehead with a dirty white handkerchief. Then he stuffed it into his back pocket, hitched up his pants, and nodded to his wife to continue.

"We got a couple of ladder-back chairs here. Need a bit of paint, but they're nice and sturdy. Just right for front-porch settin'. Let's start 'em off at ten bucks. Two times the money."

Alice struggled to hold up one of the chairs while Bob held up the other. They looked to her like they needed less paint, not more. The thick green enamel had blistered and peeled; the flakes came off on her damp hands.

She looked at the couple. She doubted they would bid on anything so shabby.

"Ten-dollar, ten-dollar, anybody give ten? Ten-dollar, ten-dollar?" The words tumbled over each other. Betty paused to draw a breath. "Who'll give five?"

Alice watched, as the mill-worker who had mocked her held up two fingers.

"Yep!" Bob barked.

"Two-dollar, two-dollar, we got two-dollar, now two-fifty, two-fifty, two-fifty, anyplace?" She paused, and then, without warning, banged the gavel. "Sold for two dollars to . . . Seth, hold up your number . . . number 34."

Alice carried her chair back to give it to the buyer. He leaned against the wall and made no move to take it from her. She avoided his eyes as she dropped it to the floor in front of him.

As she returned to the front, Alice saw Bob reach behind the podium. When he handed her the unicorn, she was expecting it. She lifted it high above her head, her thin arms trembling with its weight.

"You break it, you buy it," he growled at her loud enough for the couple to hear.

Her lips etched themselves into a determined line as she raised it even higher. He meant it, she knew. Once before, she had broken a small statue and he had taken it out of her pay. But that was all right. She supposed it was fair. And anyway, it had only cost her two dollars. Most of the stuff Bob sold was real cheap, except for the unicorn. She knew she mustn't break the porcelain piece. It had cost Bob thirty dollars, and besides, it was her favorite. She lowered her aching arms and hugged the unicorn tightly, as the bidding began once again.

"This is a quality piece here. Made in England. Quality piece. You won't find nary 'nother like it."

Alice knew the bidding would start at fifty dollars. She watched as the blonde woman whispered to her companion. He raised his hand high enough for Bob to see and nodded his head, smiling.

"Yep." Bob acknowledged the bid.

Alice raised the unicorn once again above her head and prayed that the couple would not get it. Looking across the room, she saw old Maud raise her arms, splaying six scrawny fingers in front of her.

The locals, wise to Bob's favorite "bait and switch," watched with knowing grins as the couple bid against old Maud, who, in return for her service as house bidder, was given small treats from the concession.

"Sixty, we have sixty. Do I hear seventy, seventy, seventy?"

The man again nodded at Bob, who stood in front of him, making beckoning motions.

Again the triumphant "Yep!"

The room pulsed with the rhythms of the auctioneer's cadence. Alice looked at old Maud, who grinned and threw up her arm.

"Yep."

"Eighty-dollar, eighty-dollar, eighty, eighty . . . do I hear ninety?"

Alice looked at the couple. The woman was whispering and nodding. The man looked thoughtful, then raised his hand.

"One hundred dollars," he said to Bob, who was still hovering in front of him.

Betty's voice boomed over the loudspeaker. "One hundred, we have one hundred. Do I hear a hundred and five? Hundred and five, anyplace? One hundred going once, going twice."

With the slam of the gavel Alice's spirits plummeted.

"Sold! For one hundred dollars to number 87."

Now was the time that the unicorn would be switched. Alice knew Bob would make a big deal about packing it and boxing it to protect its fragile horn. He would even tape it before handing it over to the unsuspecting customer, who would usually not bother to unwrap and inspect it on the spot. The one time it had been opened and examined, Bob had made a big fuss about the "mistake," blamed it on his "helpers," and apologized loudly. His helpers, he had said, had

142

broken the other one in packing, and since they didn't always recognize "a quality piece," had assumed the substitution would be all right. "I reckon they figure you seen one unicorn you seen 'em all." He had laughed loudly, given the customer back his money, and quickly gone on with the auction.

One other time a customer had attempted to return the worthless figurine several days later and Bob had gruffly referred him to the sign that read "All Sales Final." The customer had left frustrated but wiser.

Alice had always followed this procedure with little interest other than a modicum of appreciation for her stepfather's cunning. Suddenly, as she stood hugging the porcelain, she realized that such dealings were shabby. Cheap. Like the auction barn itself. Embarrassed and a little frightened by this newly acquired knowledge, she was an enlightened Eve looking for a fig-leaf.

Alice felt her face redden and her palms begin to sweat. She glanced down at the unicorn, felt the smoothness of its surface, fingered the graceful curves of its horn, where she knew the magic was supposed to be. She raised her eyes to focus on the couple who had bought, or at least thought they had bought, a quality piece.

The woman was reaching out her hands, eager to examine and exult over her bargain, her "find" in this country backwater.

From the corner of her eye Alice saw Bob step forward to reclaim the lovely object for packaging. He would whisk it away and make the switch. It was now or never.

Alice knew what she had to do. She did it quickly and without hesitation. She did it with the fresh impulsiveness of youth. She didn't stop to think about the "whuppin" that she would surely get or how many times five dollars would go into a hundred. She didn't stop to mull the moral ethic or contemplate the philosophical principle.

She gave a jerky breath and dropped her blue eyes to the floor. The porcelain unicorn lay in fragments at her feet. On her face was a look of triumph, and still echoing in her ears, the startling sound of breaking glass, bouncing in the air.

She bent down and carefully extracted the horn from the jagged rubble. Once again, she fingered it lovingly. By some miracle it had emerged whole, unblemished, its magic still intact, a confirmation, she reasoned, of her rashness. It was an omen. She would keep its magic forever with her.

Alice squared her shoulders and smiled at the couple. The perplexed expression on the woman's face told her that her act of courage would go unremarked and unappreciated. She looked up, directly into Bob's scowl of disbelief. He had started toward her, but she knew he wouldn't hit her in front of everybody. That might come later, but it didn't matter. Alice slipped the talisman into her pocket and turned to face the wrath to come. As she did so she heard old Maud chuckle.

"Yessiree Bob, you got yerself a quality piece there."

Maura's Vision

A Veri-tale by Nina Silver

PART ONE

(Ia) *

Seeing through Maura is like peering through a crystal. Everything is clear, but flat, the kind of perspective she and other humans have when they watch a movie. It's not as easy to see the Earth plane through Maura's husband Alan; the circuits in his brain that allow for a clear visual sometimes get a little muddy. But feeling through his body is another story.

* In your dimension, where thoughts and words are usually vocalized, my name would be pronounced, "Eeya."

The striations of muscle are smooth, flowing, the feeling you get when you visit a stream in the mountains. Allen has a very strong body, the kind of strength I would like to have if I were in his dimension.

Sometimes Maura and Alan go to the movies, and, naturally, I watch. The screen comes alive with sights that are for me twice removed; after all, it is a third-hand visual, having passed through the camera's eye and Maura's sight before entering my own field of perception. Viewing with the two of them has always been fun. I look through Maura's eyes and split my beam so that part of me projects through Alan's body, feeling the warmth of skin as they hold hands.

Alan was a very difficult human to hone in on at first. He did not provide the easy, unwitting access that Maura always seemed to claim as part of her nature. Perhaps this was because, unlike Maura, Alan rarely lost his composure. A hard, efficient manner allowed one only to contemplate what lay beneath.

A short time ago, however, he and Maura experienced some difficulties which altered his state of receptivity to a marked degree. They began having the most distressing fights.

148

It is not in my nature to be a voyeur. In my form I can travel to far corners of the universe and back again in an instant, and I am not at a loss for companionship. There are no dearer friends than the other dimensional beings who live, vibrate, and visit in the same manner as myself; and our explorations to different dimensions, and the knowledge gained there about ourselves and others, have always been very satisfying. Therefore, I feel somewhat at a loss at times to explain why I have chosen Maura and Alan—two beings extraordinarily different from myself, and at times inordinately difficult—as intelligences I would want to spend time with. I suppose it must be sufficient to say that I love them both, and leave it at that.

I had been on the outskirts of their lives, quiet and unintrusive, for a relatively short while. I was grateful for whatever companionship they unknowingly provided me, and through the channels of very deep and subtle communication I always made sure to send them light. I figured it could only help to make them feel a little happier.

Alas, when you are an unseen and uninvited guest, no matter how good your intentions might be, the invisibility ultimately begins to be wearing. I began to wonder if my presence could contribute anything of lasting worth to either them or myself. Indeed, I had started questioning my intrinsic usefulness, when their fighting became particularly intense. They began to experience problems in bed.

PART TWO

(Maura)

"Come on, honey," Alan cajoled. His muscular arms tugged beneath the cover and I pulled away, trying to get more air.

"C'mon." This way Alan has of insisting, as if he's the only person who counts, has always gotten on my nerves. Tonight I found it more grating than usual.

"No!" The power of my own voice startled me. I looked around uneasily, to see if anyone else were in the room.

"Maura, what *is* your problem?" Even though Alan didn't move, I knew from the way his skin started to cool that he was pulling back. I rested my chin in my hands and watched him. He met my gaze, stonily.

"Look, Alan," I finally said, "it's just that when you're so . . . "

"So . . . what?"

I took a deep breath and began again. "Whenever we've had sex lately, you act like it's just another day in court. You're not at work, for heaven's sake. Don't you know that making love isn't a matter of negotiation? I can't stand it when you try to convince me with this 'If you make love with me you'll be glad' business. Two people do it because they want to, not because the other person will be nice to them if they give in."

I wondered why Alan let me go on for as long as I did without interrupting. Then I realized how acutely my remark had struck him; every muscle in his body had stiffened, as though braced for an attack.

"Alan?" He turned away, a thin but very loaded layer of air between us. My eyes swelled and my mouth opened to form words; but all I could do was stammer, as if nothing I said would make a difference, "Alan . . . please!"

He turned back to me with eyes like a hurt puppy's. "Please, what?"

"Alan, for God's sake, talk to me. Come on. You know I hate going to bed like this. I never get a good night's sleep when we fight."

"Hell, Maura, you can sleep during the day. I have a job, remember?"

My face started to burn. It wasn't as though I hadn't been looking for work. But every time I was offered a position, I backed out. Something inside kept saying, "This isn't right. Wait." But wait for what?

Alan spoke as if he had read my mind. "What are you waiting for, Princess? An engraved invitation and a limousine to pick you up? Meanwhile, I'm sweating my guts out."

That did it. I grabbed the nearest pillow and slugged him with it. Alan was so surprised, he just lay there and stared at me for what must have been a full minute. It felt like an eternity.

Finally, I broke the silence. "Just because I don't have a job, that doesn't give you the right to treat me like this. What am I supposed to do, have sex with you in exchange for living here? I'm not trying to avoid doing my share. I just need more time. . . . I can't explain it." I turned away, biting down on my trembling lower lip.

"Listen, Maura"—Alan sounded genuinely contrite—"I'm sorry. That was unfair of me. It's just . . . well, sometimes I don't know how to . . . what I mean is . . . Maura, please."

He reached over awkwardly and took my hand. His arm felt warm and slightly tingling, as though a small current were pulsing through it. The sensation was a little strange to me, but I kept holding his hand anyway. As I looked back at him, trying to understand, I realized that Alan didn't seem to feel totally comfortable with the sensation either.

His whole body gradually overflowed with the charge, as though all his inner warmth were being pushed to the surface by some bright sun, that was bathing each cell, every pore of skin. It was this inner warmth that had made me fall in love with him and which I so terribly missed. Why had things between us changed so? But tonight, as this warmth softly enveloped us and the muscles in Alan's tense back started to relax, the same electricity began to flow through me. The words Alan still had not spoken formed his caress. And as we started to embrace with our entire bodies, we each knew what the other for so long had wanted to say.

PART THREE

(Ia)

Imagine your energy being drawn out like salt water taffy, the chewiest kind, between two people, who playfully vie for the biggest piece. I felt that my form was expanding, lengthening, deepening in intensity. My emotions were growing, too. The crystal clarity of Maura's visionary field remained constant. But as I continued to stay with the two of them, I perceived in Alan a greater openness to me, as well as more depth in the flow between him and Maura. I began to feel more alive, happy that at last I could be of value to two humans who would never be able to see me, at least not as they were at present.

PART FOUR

(Maura)

I met Alan when I was twenty-six, in the dinosaur room of the natural history museum. I was half-heartedly trying to sketch a Tyrannosaurus Rex, which he remarked would be better off remaining in its showcase. After that, we were inseparable.

Perhaps I should have considered his proposal of marriage more carefully. It wasn't that I didn't love Alan; he was funny and warm, and we shared many interests and ways of viewing the world. But I had never been to college or traveled much. And I had no career to speak of, only a boring secretarial job which I hated. In short, there wasn't anything that I felt was special about my life or that gave it much purpose or meaning. So I weakened. It was hard not to. As with most things that he felt strongly about, Alan was very insistent on marrying me. And as with most things that Alan wanted, I caved in and agreed.

Still, though, I wondered if there wasn't something I should do first, some experience I needed to go through. But what? In the end, any misgivings I had about getting married were dismissed; the wedding was a full-time project that demanded my undivided attention. I gratefully quit my job and threw myself into all the usual ceremonial details, while Alan, after thoroughly investigating bank loans, put his entire savings into a down payment on a small three-bedroom house. Not wanting to waste any time, we moved in immediately.

But soon all that planning and frenzied activity was ancient history. The wedding had faded into a dream, the last of the boxes were unpacked, and Alan and I had established a routine. Suddenly, I felt empty. True, Alan and I were getting along better now, but there was no guarantee how long this renewed connection would last. And I still couldn't bring myself to take an outside job.

Yet I had to do something. I couldn't just sit home, staring at the walls. Much to my surprise, I began to reminisce about the serious art classes I had taken as a teenager. An old desire surged through me, of being an accomplished painter.

"It's too hard," Dad used to say, when I'd be earnestly painting and dreaming, "to compete in the art field. If I were a woman, Maura, I'd take it easy. You're pretty. If you play your cards right, you can have the pick of any man you want. Why bother with a career?" And he'd wink at me confidentially, as if sharing a special trick to living your life that no one else was supposed to know. Mom, a discreet woman with a perpetual smile, did not disagree, so I thought Dad had to be right.

But now a stranger seemed to be inhabiting this married woman's body, my body. After staying home day after day, nervously pacing from room to room, I began to find fault with our little house.

The house cried out for transformation, something lovely and kind, to help people feel as though they truly belonged in it. So for the next month, while Alan was at his job, I worked at mine, even though mine didn't pay a salary. Deciding that there was nothing more important than creating a harmonious environment, I plunged into the task of redecorating the house. I was relieved at the opportunity at last to exercise some artistic talent, even if it was only for interior design.

But eventually, there was nothing left to do. The number of walls to paper was finite, every last mirror and picture that could be crammed into our cozy space was hung, and it became redundant to rearrange the furniture. I was more restless and bored than ever, illogically resenting Alan for leaving me alone in that desolate, decorated house. After nearly going crazy from having nothing redeeming or inspiring to do, I was flooded by an overwhelming desire to paint.

I didn't *want* to want to paint. Being an artist was an ambition I thought was safely tucked away with a past that was no longer mine. I was certain to be rusty; I hadn't held a brush in years. But after doing nothing for five whole weeks except mope over the lost time that I could have spent painting, I decided to see what, if anything, of myself I could salvage. I went out and bought some canvas and materials, and started to experiment.

The landscapes I had done in my teens, though well crafted, had been otherwise quite ordinary. Now, my fascination with color rendered those early paintings invisible. I painted scenes that I whimsically thought could not have been of this earth—they were far too rich and expansive. The whites and blues, the yellows, and especially the golds, had enormous depth; they suggested other forms and color that were not there. Even the shadows were luminescent. Most important, though, I gave myself permission to close my eyes and dream, for therein lay the paintings.

Yet compared to what I saw in my visions, applying brush to canvas still seemed like a feeble afterthought, a poor conveyor of realms I could not quite reach. Frustrated that my paintings could not express the elusive imagery of my mind's eye, I sometimes painted right through dinner, and Alan, home from work and hungry, would yell because I hadn't prepared anything. I would apologize later, after we had both had a chance to eat and settle down; he from feeling tired and unappreciated, I from an inner world so vivid that I had to struggle to relate to the outer one.

Surprising myself, and worrying Alan greatly, I became a total recluse, exiting the spare room studio primarily for meals (which I eventually learned to get ready on time). I socialized with friends only under threat of losing them if I didn't, or when Alan manipulated our schedule in such a way that I couldn't say no. I left the house only to shop for food or to rejuvenate myself with sunlight, getting primed for my next picture.

Gradually, Alan's concern about my hermit-like behavior dissolved, as the number of paintings grew. He no longer said a word about my not having a "real" job; in fact, he made a point of telling all his friends and colleagues that his wife was an artist. Nothing thrilled me more than when he would ask questions about where I got my ideas, though I must admit that most of the time I couldn't tell him.

It was on a chilly autumn evening that his presence in the painting-studded foyer actually got me to come out of the studio.

"Now," he chided me in a gentle, bemused way, seeing he had his chance, "what planet is that?"

"Which?"

"This one"—pointing his finger—"with all the funny-looking . . . what are they, bananas? . . . bananas, running around. Yeah, they must be bananas, they're yellow."

"Alan!" I protested, laughing, "that's gold. And they're not bananas. They're"—I hurriedly searched for something they could be, and found it—"beams of light. Don't you know light when you see it?"

"Hmmm. I don't see light, only bananas. Very peculiar, doing very un-banana-like things. But bananas nonetheless. Prancing around with other like-minded bananas. Speaking of food, all this talk is making me hungry. We got any fruit?"

"Alan!"

"Come here, Maura. Tell me, how do you come up with these images? I haven't even seen them in sci-fi films. You could sell to Star Flight Fantasy Productions or some such conglomerate and clean up." He paused, trying one last shot. "Are you sure these aren't interplanetary bananas?" As he gazed at me, my body felt like hot wax, each part dripping into the next.

I threw my arms around him. "Alan," I declared, striving unsuccessfully to prevent the corners of my mouth from turning up, "those aren't from anywhere except my own brilliant, fertile mind. It's called imagination. When was the last time you ate? All you ever think of is food."

It turned out Alan had something more serious on his mind than bananas.

"Maura," he began, later that night after we'd gotten into bed and folded down the quilt in one motion, "how about getting your work out? Start going around to galleries. You've painted a whole roomful of canvases, not counting the ones we've hung."

I was silent.

"Well?" Alan looked right at me, his searching blue eyes reflecting the glow from the night-lit sky, filled with its own secrets and globular life forms. I couldn't speak. I didn't have any formal training in being a professional anything, much less in marketing what I thought was a most unprofessionally developed talent.

But I knew Alan was right: these paintings were what I had been waiting for, and now it was time to let others see them. The prospect of doing that scared me, much more than I wanted to admit. Still, I couldn't help but smile under Alan's unblinking eyes, that poured through me like an endless peaceful river. He leaned over to brush my neck with his lips and my skin opened. Then the rest of me opened to him, and to the whitely luminescent moon, kissing its way down the drapes to make spiraled patterns on his back.

PART FIVE

(Ia)

My dimension is a very bright place, filled with music of the spheres, and flowing with color and laughter that usually cannot be perceived on the Earth plane. My favorite times are when I contact my best cronies and seek other galaxies to explore. When that is not possible, nothing pleases me more than having the lightning-like conversations that characterize telepathic communion.

It is somewhat difficult to engage in such communion when all your concentration is directed toward sending light to the Earth plane. This had been a particularly taxing time for me. I was pouring huge amounts of energy into trying to help those two humans cooperate with one another, and now I was a constant in Maura's visual field. When I felt isolated, it helped to think about nearby dimensions and some of the adventures I had shared with others who were like me.

I had not been in contact with another dimensional being for what even to me seemed like a long time. It was therefore a great surprise one afternoon, when I was doing what I usually do—thinking of my dimension in all its light forms, while beaming some love to the earth plane—that I sensed an unusual energy pattern circling through Maura's right brain.

What is this? I thought to myself, zooming in for a closer look. *She seems even more open than usual. Not only is reception better, but in some subtle way I think she knows I'm here.*

You can imagine my shock to receive an answer: *That's because I have a stronger charge than you, which has helped open her up even more. I've been with Maura for about three weeks.*

I honed in onto a faster vibration. *Funny,* I again thought to myself, *I didn't notice this one before.*

True to our manner as dimensional beings, of instantaneous contact once the connection is made, my musing was answered: *That's because you've been busy working through particular circuits and haven't touched others. I have a much different approach than you. You see, I am not from an Earth dimension.*

Telepathically, we were hooked up quite strongly now, and I had a much better sense of a very loving and strong soul. *How did you come to connect with her?* I was eager to find out.

Because she needed additional input, and I felt drawn to her. Don't worry, you opened her to my charge, I see that now. There's no reason to feel you've done a second-rate job. Would you like to see how I link with her mind?

I watched, fascinated, through a jumble of refractive light, as my new friend demonstrated the different manner of sending to Maura. She also conveyed the name I was to indicate when I wished to connect: *Shereen.*

I like that name, I beamed. *I don't like to be noted as anything except "Ia."*

That's easy, my friend flashed. *Does Maura know your name?*

No. She doesn't even know I exist.

Shereen paused, scanning Maura's visual centers to view the canvas she was working on. *Yet she suggests our forms and depicts our dimensions.* We absorbed an impression of a bright painting similar to the one Alan maintained had bananas in it. *I like this one,* Shereen gleamed. *It looks very much like where we are.*

I peered through particular circuitry to get a closer look. *So it does. I've been sending to her constantly.*

You see, then, it is not exactly true that she doesn't know you. Maura's vision is really quite advanced.

But the levels on which we touch are very subtle.

Then you must get lonely. The amplitude of Shereen's vibration reached out to mine.

Yes. I feel it even more now that you're here. I sighed in a fashion recognizable only to another dimensional being. *It's been a while since I've communed like this.*

Shereen understood well. *I have been to many dimensions not of this planet, and the time is right for me to visit again. Would you like to come with me?*

But she needs me. She is painting. I hesitated to leave my self-appointed guardianship.

You don't need to spend as much time with her as you used to. She and Alan are getting along better now. Also, she knows, Shereen pointed out. *And she knows that she knows, even if she can't yet identify what it is that she knows. Do you really think she won't be able to paint if you leave her alone for a while?* Shereen's golden frequency rippled a bit faster. *She has linked well. She will still be able to receive light, even if no one is specifically sending. The connection is too strong at this point for her to close herself to it.*

I considered what Shereen had just conveyed. *Where are you going?* I wanted to know.

There is this planet with four suns, and hookup between it and its astral planes is unique. I think you may learn something to bring back here and use.

The prospect of sending better to both Maura and Alan appealed to me greatly; and besides, I had heard about this particular planet before and always wondered how it could orbit in such a way that there was never a spot that was not receiving energy from at least one of the four suns.

In a flash Shereen and I were gone.

There are myriad different dimensions within each sphere of rarefied atmosphere surrounding what have become known as planets. The million or so where I have personally taken my entire self, not the ones to which I have simply made long distance telepathic calls, are as different from each other as Maura is from Alan. Needless to say, one's imagination is promptly tested.

We arrived there in an instant, greatly enjoying each other's light, accepting companionship. Our first order of business was to send out feelers, to see which of the four-sun astral planes could offer us both the most hospitable clime.

I was in between dimensional vibrations, one slightly faster than the next, when I heard a low buzz. Immediately, something bright flashed into my field, and I knew I was about to meet one of the native inhabitants of this dimension.

The accompanying laughter—if you can imagine it as such, since in our forms there is no physical mechanism to utter sounds—was of such clarity and depth that I couldn't help but respond in kind. Smack in front of my field of awareness there glowed . . . no, that is much too subdued a term . . . there *illuminated* this being of such gentleness and joy that if I could have gasped for breath, I would have.

Mith is my name. The words rumbled easily into my consciousness. *I see you are from the planet Earth.*

In a twinkling Shereen was at my side. Mith had so much fire and such an unusually fluid manner that for several moments Shereen and I merely took in the uniqueness of this vibration, the way the space around Mith had of sympathetically paralleling the density of energy at certain points in the cycle of movement.

Welcome, Mith graciously extended, pulsating like some tiny, magnificent beacon. *Let us go where you will both be comfortable. You're not originally from Earth, are you?–* to Shereen.

No.

Then it will have to be a dimension that will accommodate your two very different energies.

We landed gently inside a gold vapor of steady humming softness. It felt so delicious, I couldn't imagine why Earth hadn't manufactured an astral plane like this.

Mith was already showing us some of the characteristics of this planet and its unique dimensions. *Here,* we were told, *extend yourselves further than you think this dimension will take you.* The moment we did, we virtually bounced from the periphery of the plane into a kind of elasticized field. This elasticization, Mith explained, was a property of all the dimensions, which overlapped into the ionosphere of the host planet. Because of this overlap (generally blue-grey, but our area happened to shine like dim crystal), we could see the planet with four suns as easily as its own inhabitants did. You can imagine my delight at having access to the material plane—*any* material plane—without needing Maura to be my eyes.

My field of vision greedily took in everything: the lush vegetation around concave pockets of nourishing liquid gas; the stretch of low, dense brush that hugged the land close where there were no pockets; the sky, blazing from all sides like a thousand iridescent candles, only brighter. Naturally, I was wildly curious about the planetary intelligence. I looked, but could find no inhabitants other than the plants.

Or maybe the vegetable life *was* the intelligence, more prone to creative awareness that I had given it credit for. I looked again. My senses told me there was a higher, unseen life we had not yet contacted.

Mith beamed to me, very quietly I thought: *The inhabitants are very timid of the astral plane beings, who, out of respect, maintain courses closer to the centers of this planet's four thousand five hundred ninety-eight dimensions. It takes trust to connect. If you are going to*

169

stay in the nearest boundaries, you must tone down your vibration.

I thought intently about what Mith had said about trust. Perhaps, with enough diligence, I could learn how to send to Maura and Alan even better, so that ultimately they would be able to meet me with total consciousness . . . and without fear.

Mith was pale now in comparison to the glow of our initial meeting. Shereen, who, having resided in Earth's astral planes, clearly understood the mechanics of my kind of flow, was a better teacher than Mith and showed me exactly how to manipulate the intensity of my form. For more than one reason I was grateful for Shereen's presence on this new, strange planet.

Once the three of us toned down, we didn't have long to wait. The—I can only call them "creatures"— appeared abruptly from the taller vegetation and slowly ambled out into the bright, clear day (though, to be sure, it was always day there by Earth standards, even when the suns were at a minimal number). The beasts were reminiscent of the model dinosaurs Alan and Maura occasionally visited in their favorite museum. They had such great, furry bodies and fierce-looking teeth and claws that I had to remind

170

myself how gentle and peace-loving they actually were. I must confess that it was difficult to imagine how those frightening beasts could possibly fear such an innocuous-looking being as myself; at times I saw no difference between me and one of their suns, my form only scaled down to the tiniest fraction. Still, there is no accounting for what makes one soul afraid and not another. Mith saw me watching the creatures play and asked Shereen and me if we wanted to try to connect with one or two of the braver ones.

I excitedly assented. Dissipating our energy as much as we could, we practically floated to a spot right above one of the gas caves. It was giving off a crackling sound as some gas began to liquefy. Nearby, a very large beast was grazing. I sensed enormous intelligence and humor in its awareness, and I knew that Mith had chosen wisely.

Between Mith and the creature a kind of opening began to tunnel itself into the atmosphere of this lovely planet, a narrow beam that ever so gently widened, filling with the most sensitively sent resonances I had ever witnessed. Mith was a master at this; I could tell that much time of reflection and effort had been given to perfecting the process. Shereen was as absorbed as I, and I tried to focus even harder, as I

171

knew I would be the slower to learn. Shereen was a much more experienced traveler than I and better psychically developed. I didn't want to be left behind in anything.

The creature raised its head from feeding and looked hard into our astral plane. It seemed to perceive more with a sixth sense, however, than it actually saw with its eyes. It was only then that I realized the advantage that Mith, Shereen, and others like myself had in our direct perception of these creatures. I wondered a bit uneasily if my shadowy presence would always be a potential cause for alarm in beings who did not possess the same faculties as myself.

Shereen started to remind me that that was why I was here, to learn how to manifest without frightening others, when our discussion was cut short by Mith.

Sssh! There's a reciprocal send in the channel.

We focused back to the material plane. Sure enough, the animal-like intelligence had received Mith's very gentle beam and was just starting to beam back a message, when I felt something tug urgently in the recesses of my mind.

PART SIX

(Maura)

The room was swirling with light, now lengthening, then compressing, sometimes circular and geodesically patterned. When my eyes finally focused, as much as they were able, the bluish-grey haze and crystal glints reluctantly pre-empted themselves to the starched whiteness that gives hospitals such a bleakly familiar character.

Hospital! What was I doing in a room the stern color of someone's apron? Then the shimmering began again, this time in spirals that, if I hadn't known better, I would have sworn were pulling me into another time.

Time . . . it seemed so irrelevant, somehow. Time was something we used to order our perceptions or map out an event. After all, what did time matter when I made love with Alan?

Alan! I sat up abruptly, but was stopped by a sharp pain in the side of my head. It was then that I realized I couldn't turn my neck to the right. Groggily, I forced my eyes to look down. Part of my body was covered with gauze, and beneath the bandages it felt as if whole sections of my skin had been ripped away. Fixing on present time filled me with a scream.

A nurse came in quickly. "How do you feel? Do you remember what happened? You've been in an automobile accident."

"Alan—is he all right? Where is he? Can I see him?" The rapid discharge of questions exhausted me. I relaxed my head, sinking into the mattress.

That good nurse was careful in her delivery. "He's on critical. You can't see him now; he's in the operating room. He was punctured by flying glass, and some internal organs were ruptured. There was quite a loss of blood. They're working on him very hard." She came closer and touched me in just the right way. "We were hoping for better news. But where there's life there's hope. Can I get you anything?"

From deep in my belly a wail emerged that seemed to resound in all the corners of the room, ricocheting to the very bowels of the universe itself. The sound reminded me of something foreign, bestial, yet familiar. It was so vast, my mind couldn't hold it all. As I focused back on my body, I found myself sobbing, feeling for the first time in my life the agonizing pain of profound loss. The nurse held me as I wept.

Inexplicably, in the face of such darkness, I sensed a vague, sheltering light.

PART SEVEN

(Ia)

The speed of my dimensional return, if I were human, would have left me short of breath. The automobile carrying Alan and Maura had bounced off the guard rail, turned over, and spun again in a one hundred eighty degree turn. The mangle of energies was perforated with pain. I felt the pain as much as any awareness in my position might, but with one difference: I felt even more keenly a sense of horror at possibly losing a loved one.

The jumbled striations of Alan's strong muscles would not decode until after he was put under anesthesia, when the fear and the disorganization could leave his force field. Maura, who I was relieved to know would live, was accessible as ever. I saw through her eyes the gash in her husband's side and felt the heaviness in her head as she tried to move it.

The fire from the engine burned hotly; it seemed to take its time—very lucky for them, since it took interminably long for three strangers to manage the task of removing the pair from the wreck. I still have no clear idea of how the accident actually occurred; but then, mechanics is not my strongest study.

Alan was in such bad shape that I had no real effect on him until he went under the anesthetic (though I tried very hard). The normally receptive channels in his brain resumed their proper function then. They never did need his conscious assent—thank goodness for that.

As the surgery proceeded, I began to feel a shift in his focus. Something was wrong: Alan was not staying in his body. The reception was still there—in fact, it was clearer than ever, but I realized, to my dismay, that this was because he was moving into my dimension.

Go back, I beamed. *This isn't your time yet.*

The Alan I was meeting at that moment seemed disoriented. *Where am I?*

You are not where you belong. Go back. Your time is not now.

He seemed to adjust to this information. *Body in much pain,* I was told. *Can't bear it. Vital signs weak.*

What about Maura? Are you going to leave the one person on your plane who really loves and understands you?

Alan's awareness shifted more strongly into my dimension. The intensity of his inner warmth could shine easily here, and I found it brighter than ever.

You . . . I know who you are now. Why haven't you made your presence known to us more clearly? The conversation between us took place almost instantaneously: we were honing in well on each other.

I did, I insisted.

Ah . . . no matter. We meet now. I felt his gratitude drift toward me like a warm cloud.

My attention turned to Alan's body. It was growing weaker. *Look,* I told him, *you have a choice. You must decide now, before that decision can no longer be made. It must be made now.*

Alan seemed reluctant. *Can I come again into your space, and will I know you when I return to the form I am trying to keep alive? I want to remember.*

I hesitated briefly. *Yes, you will know. But now I must ask you to go. Know that I love you both, and have been sending you much light.*

Alan's leg muscles began to twitch as his focus became whole. His midsection had already been stitched. A second team of surgeons, concentrating furiously, was at his right side. It felt terrible to beam through it, but I did anyway, hoping that some of the new sending techniques I had just learned might possibly help. After all, when you have been with someone for a while, it is very easy to become attached.

PART EIGHT

(Alan)

Maura was restless and highly distraught. Something was bothering her besides the fact that I had almost died.

Not that I begrudged her; indeed, I understood her mood very well because I was feeling depressed myself. Every one of Maura's paintings had been in the burning car at the time of the accident, due for delivery to a gallery show that never happened. I felt a deep loss that I couldn't explain; and since it was unexplainable, I didn't discuss it.

If Maura was devastated, she tried not to show it. Instead, she fussed over me with such single-minded attention that I might have yelled at her, had I not also been preoccupied with the loss of her paintings.

They seemed to call to me, taunt me with their diffusely lit worlds I could almost have touched . . . but when? Why did they seem more real than the bed I lay in? And how could I reach those realms again?

Maura's voice gradually filled my consciousness. She had been calling my name for a while.

I shook myself, as much as was possible in my leaden, aching body. "Yes, honey?" A smile effortlessly formed on my lips. She *was* my honey, and I was finding it much easier to let her know that. A lot of things felt easier these days . . . and so different.

"Alan, are you all right? You seem so distant, remote . . . as if . . . as if you're looking for something."

"Hmmm, I suppose I am." I took her hand and held it against my cheek.

"Alan—Maura was trembling—"I get scared when you go away."

"Honey, I'm right here." I gripped her hand tighter.

Maura started to cry. "When you go off into space, I'm afraid you're not coming back!"

A tear splashed onto my chest. Startled, I realized it was mine. "No, Maura, I'm staying. I promise. For a long time." Very slowly, I moved my body, which hurt like hell, to make room for her on the bed. We held each other for a long time without speaking.

"Alan."

"Yes, Maura."

"Alan, I miss them."

"I know. So do I." I paused. "But you can paint others."

Maura's gaze bore right through me with the immensity of the grief she had been trying to hide. "No, I can't," she sobbed.

"You will," I said quickly, "even better ones. Talent isn't something you lose. I know you'll paint again. Give yourself some time."

I surprised myself with the authority of my words. Maura gazed at me again, wanting to believe, and suddenly there was light, a tremendous well of luminous golden light, that began to carry me to other places, just as her paintings had. Time and motion were suspended. After an indeterminable length of time, I jerked out of the reverie into which I had fallen. A pleasant warm tingling, which was by now a familiar and old friend, was passing between the two of us like an electric current. Only now it was stronger than ever. It reminded me of Maura's paintings, and I felt happy.

"It'll be all right, honey. I promise." Maura's eyes and my own reflected each other's, like two deep pools. "Maura, I'm remembering. When I was on the operating table, I had a vision. I saw what you must have seen that made you want to paint."

As if in accord, a dim sensation of light met the periphery of my ocular field, although what exactly it was, I could not quite grasp. Immediately, I could tell that Maura saw it too, and that she knew, whatever had been lost with her paintings she would find again.

PART NINE

(Ia)

I am a particle of gold light. That does not, however, tell you as much about me as does my relationship with Maura and Alan, for usually, when a soul is out of its body in a dimension other than the material, there is fear on the part of the humans. But in expanding my ability to communicate, I have made it possible for Alan and Maura to feel much more comfortable with me. This is relatively rare.

In truth, there is really nothing alarming about communicating with a particle of light, and I am very comfortable with my form. Still, I suppose that if I were again in what you might call a body, and met another being like myself as I am now, it would be a probable cause for alarm.

However, it is not my form which is the most important point to make, but, rather, my relationship to the individuals with whom I connect. For when you are constantly with someone, you eventually grow to love them, and it is very easy to become attached.

Biographical Sketches

a brief introduction to the authors and designers of
VeriTales: Note of Hope

Bruce Burrows was born in the small desert town of Ridgecrest, California, but he associates both his own growth and that of his writing with the Naropa Institute of Boulder, Colorado, where he is currently an M.F.A. candidate in Writing and Poetics. His humorous but insightful story, "A Very Safe Man," reflects the Naropa commitment "to explore and cultivate mindfulness and awareness as basic elements in the practice of writing." Bruce's fiction has appeared in BOMBAY GIN, THE LITTLE MAGAZINE, and THE THINKER REVIEW; his poetry in MAN ALIVE, BOMBAY GIN, INTER/FACE, and ABOLISH.

Judith Davey, born in Germany and having lived in England, Canada, and now the United States, brings to her writing a lifetime of multi-cultural experiences. Now retired, she devotes her time to sharing those experiences through the written word. "Four in the Blast" conveys the unspoken intimacy of strangers. That concept may be foreign to those accustomed to the easy anonymity of peacetime. It will strike chords of familiarity, however, to those who, like Judith, caught in the horror of war, have personally faced the possibility of death shared with strangers. Judith's stories have been published in VINTAGE NORTHWEST and READ ME, and her book, OUTSIDERS LOOKING IN, won a Pacific Northwest Writers Conference award in 1991.

Susan Ito has been active in the Committee for Health Rights in Central America since her first visit to Nicaragua in 1984. In 1989 she quit working as a physical therapist to become newsletter editor and programs coordinator for CHRICA. In annual trips for CHRICA she encountered the thousands of "street children" of Central America and experienced the seeds for "The Price of Limes in Managua." Susan is currently an M.F.A. candidate in Creative Writing at Mills College in Oakland, California. Her fiction and non-fiction have appeared in NEW DIRECTIONS FOR WOMEN, AMERICAN WAY MAGAZINE, HURRICANE ALICE, and numerous anthologies.

Robert Montgomery's resume might be longer than his short fiction. Journalist, high school English teacher, construction worker, assistant theatrical producer, European vagabond, naturalist, author, photographer, editor, he draws on his diverse experience to create stories which, in his words, "reflect growth and might help readers get along in life." His work as senior writer/conservation for BASSMASTER MAGAZINE has recently taken him to Costa Rica, Nicaragua, and Venezuela, where his activities ranged from visiting isolated Indian villages to fishing for piranha. For the past three years he has written all of the copy and taken many of the photographs for the highly acclaimed annual publication, LIVING WATERS, which has received "Take Pride in America" recognition from the Department of the Interior.

John Nesbitt teaches English and Spanish at Eastern Wyoming College in Torrington, Wyoming. John is widely recognized as a knowledgeable spokesman for the West. His fiction, non-fiction, poetry, and literary articles have been published in anthologies, magazines, and literary journals throughout the western United States and have received numerous prizes and awards, including a Wyoming Arts Council literary fellowship for his fiction writing. John's work addresses those "few things we all have in common—we are born, we love, we have hopes and disillusionments, we die." He expresses the purpose for his writing: "Sometimes another person's story enlightens our own, and with that hope we read and we listen."

David Shapiro, whose story, "Poor Devil," appeared in VERITALES - RING OF TRUTH, again applies his searching philosophical mind to create the deeply insightful "Harvest." He describes this story, alternately entitled "Reaper," as being "about Piaget, and the need for differentiation to create individuation. Or it's about death and life, loss and integrity." David is also one of our dedicated "environmentalist authors," having achieved, in the editorial process, a record number of re-uses of a single floppy disk mailer. With this type of author, our minds and our forests will continue to grow.

Janet Schumer, of Maywood, New Jersey, is an avid mystery writer. However, her writing experience is utterly diverse. She served as editor of Souvenirs and Novelties, a trade publication; she has edited several weekly newspapers and worked as a writer for the National Association of Private Psychiatric Hospitals. She has also taught creative writing for adults and has written all the promotional material for the Hackensack Chamber of Commerce, which she served as executive director. Her work has been published in a wide variety of magazines, ranging from LONDON MYSTERY SELECTIONS to TRAVEL MAGAZINE to DOGS IN CANADA to GOLF DIGEST to WOMEN'S WORLD.

Nina Silver is a Reichian therapist, Reiki healer, singer, composer, and writer. Her work on feminism, sexuality, the natural sciences, and metaphysics has appeared in GNOSIS, OFF OUR BACKS, THE NEW INTERNATIONALIST, GREEN EGG, JEWISH CURRENTS, and a number of feminist anthologies, including CLOSER TO HOME: BISEXUALITY AND FEMINISM, CALL IT COURAGE, CHILDLESS BY CHOICE, and WOMEN'S GLIB. Her book of poetry, BIRTHING, will be released in 1994. She describes her goal as an artist, "to provide such an organic fusion of spirituality and sexuality that my work will be perceived not as proselytizing, but as art."

Tom Traub, who grew up in Marin County, California, has a graduate degree in writing from the University of Southern California. He lives with his wife Ginny in Los Angeles, writing and working in the movie business. His short stories and poems have been published in periodicals which he describes as "as numerous as they are obscure," some of the better known of which include LIBIDO, THE CAPE ROCK, THE SILVER WEB, and the PACIFIC SUN. Tom summarizes the theme of "Becoming the Chief" in these words: "The only people who should have power are those mature enough not to want it."

Brenda Vantrease is a "daughter of the South" whose love of literature drew her to teaching. With a Bachelor's degree from Belmont University and a Master's and Doctorate from Middle Tennessee State University, she taught for twenty-five years with the Metropolitan Nashville School System. Not surprisingly, much of her writing reflects her years of working with children. The slightly different perspective which makes her writing unique is her conviction that "children are capable of both wisdom and moral courage . . . and that we can learn from their examples." Such an example is the theme of her story, "A Quality Piece."

It has taken the committed expertise of many skilled professionals to produce this anthology of veri-tales. **Steve Kaufman** of Oregon Bookbinding created the mock hardcovers which, with the artistry of photographer **Russ Illig** and cover designer **Roger Hillman**, were magically transformed into a quality trade paperback book. Roger also created the interior artwork for *Note of Hope*. We appreciate both the expertise of **Thomson-Shore, Inc.** and their commitment to the use of recycled paper in manufacturing both the first and the second titles in the *VeriTales* series.

Once again, to **Helen Wirth** goes credit for that insightful editorial wisdom that caused *New Age Journal* to describe the writing of *VeriTales* as "informed by an understated expertise in human nature."

The Hope of *VeriTales* Continues ...

This source of wonder and personal triumph has not ended just because you have turned the last page. *Note of Hope,* is the second in the on-going series of *VeriTales* anthologies. The next book, *VeriTales: Beyond the Norm,* continues where *Note of Hope* and *Ring of Truth* leave off.

On the pages that follow, you will find the Expanded Table of Contents for *VeriTales: Beyond the Norm.* Take a moment to read these brief notes about the upcoming veri-tales. Let the hope continue in your life. Place your advance order today.

Table of Contents

VeriTales: Beyond the Norm

Available May 1, 1994

traced on com

VeriTales: Beyond the Norm will be available through select bookstores and direct from the publisher, Fall Creek Press.

To order direct, call:

Toll-free 1-800-964-1905

Monday thru Thursday, 9:00-5:00 PST. Please have your VISA or MasterCard ready.

Or mail your order, including the following information:

   Name and shipping address (typed or printed clearly)

   Daytime telephone number

   Name of book(s) and how many of each

   VeriTales: Beyond the Norm @ *$14.95*

   (Available May, 1994)

   VeriTales: Note of Hope @ $14.95

   VeriTales: Ring of Truth @ 14.95

   Enclose $2.00 per book shipping/handling within U.S.

   On orders of 3 books or more, shipping/ handling within the United States is FREE.

Mail advance orders to:

   Fall Creek Press
   P.O. Box 1127
   Fall Creek, OR 97438